Also by Ian Rankin

IAN RANKIN
& SIMON READE
REBUS:
A GAME CALLED MALICE

A PLAY IN TWO ACTS

ORION

First published in Great Britain in 2023 by Orion Fiction,
an imprint of The Orion Publishing Group Ltd.,
Carmelite House, 50 Victoria Embankment
London EC4Y 0DZ

An Hachette UK Company

1 3 5 7 9 10 8 6 4 2

Rebus: A Game Called Malice was first performed at Queen's Theatre
Hornchurch on 2nd February 2023. Produced by Queen's Theatre
Hornchurch in association with Daniel Schumann and Lee Dean.

A CIP catalogue record for this book is
available from the British Library.

ISBN (Hardback) 978 1 3987 2113 5
ISBN (eBook) 978 1 3987 2114 2

Typeset at The Spartan Press Ltd,
Lymington, Hants

Printed and bound in Great Britain by Clays Ltd,
Elcograf S.p.A.

MIX
Paper from
responsible sources
FSC® C104740

www.orionbooks.co.uk

Ian Rankin is the multi-million copy worldwide bestseller of over thirty novels and creator of John Rebus. His books have been translated into thirty-six languages and have been adapted for radio, the stage and the screen.

Rankin is the recipient of four Crime Writers' Association Dagger Awards, including the Diamond Dagger, the UK's most prestigious award for crime fiction. In the United States, he has won the celebrated Edgar Award and been shortlisted for the Anthony Award. In Europe, he has won Denmark's Palle Rosenkrantz Prize, the French Grand Prix du Roman Noir and the German Deutscher Krimipreis.

He is the recipient of honorary degrees from universities across the UK, is a Fellow of the Royal Society of Edinburgh and a Fellow of the Royal Society of Literature, and has received an OBE for his services to literature. In 2022 he received a knighthood as part of the Queen's Platinum Jubilee celebrations.

Website: IanRankin.net
Twitter: @Beathhigh
Facebook: IanRankinBooks

Simon Reade is an award-winning dramatist whose feature films include the critically acclaimed *Journey's End* (director Saul Dibb, Lionsgate/BFI), and the ground-breaking *Private Peaceful* (director Pat O'Connor, Goldcrest). A frequent collaborator with Michael Morpurgo, Simon's hit theatre adaptations of the war stories include *An Elephant In The Garden, Toro! Toro!* and the international touring sensation *Private Peaceful* which has played Hong Kong, Australia, Dublin, off-Broadway, theatres across the UK and London's West End. Previous theatre collaborations include the Royal Shakespeare Company productions of Ted Hughes' *Tales From Ovid* and Salman Rushdie's *Midnight's Children* (both with Tim Supple), and *Epitaph For The Official Secrets Act* (with Paul Greengrass). Adaptations for Theatre Royal Bath Productions include *Sherlock Holmes: The Final Curtain* (starring Robert Powell), EM Forster's *A Room With A View* (starring Felicity Kendall) and *Pride & Prejudice* (subsequently revived at Regents Park/Sheffield Crucible/Guthrie Theater Minneapolis). He is the author of *Dear Mr. Shakespeare: Letters to A Jobbing Playwright* (Oberon).

CHARACTERS

John Rebus Early-to-mid 60s. A retired police detective. Dogged, socially awkward.

Stephanie Jeffries A lawyer in her late 40s/early 50s. Refined and self-confident. She has invited Rebus to be her 'plus one' tonight.

Harriet Godwin Around the same vintage as Stephanie. She comes from old money. Apparently diffident but with a core of steel. She is hosting tonight's dinner party.

Paul Godwin Harriet's husband – her second. He is around her age, maybe a year or two younger or older. He, too, comes from money, though probably not 'old' money. His parents would have been professional people, sending their son to the right schools where advancement could be assured. He is in finance of some nebulous kind.

Jack Fleming In his mid-to-late-fifties. He has worked his way up from unpromising roots, by dint of cunning, venality and muscle. He is stocky, still pugnacious, handsome in a chiselled way. He owns nightclubs and at least one casino. A sharp dresser; a ladies' man.

Candida Jones Young (late 20s?), glamorous and prone to show off her body in somewhat skimpy clothing. She describes herself as an 'influencer' and seems to live most of her life online. But she was also educated privately and possesses shrewdness and intellect.

Act One

We open in the drawing room of a palatial Georgian-era house in Edinburgh's wealthy New Town. A meal has just finished. Some detritus remains but not much – maybe a bowl of fruit. The table however boasts an array of glasses and bottles: Champagne, red wine and white, a carafe of water. Probably port and sherry too, with whisky or brandy to come.

The characters are seated around the table – except for REBUS *who prowls the room as if taking inventory.* CANDIDA *has her face in her phone screen, merrily texting away, maybe primping and taking the occasional pouting selfie. The room has two doors, one at either end. The walls are covered with works of art showing Parisian boulevards, white beaches/blue seas, still lifes of flowers in vases. These are of the Scottish colourist school (S. J. Peploe is a good comparison). There is also a large bookcase which will be perused by* REBUS, *a sofa or chaise longue, and an occasional table on which sits a floral display, still in its elaborate wrapping from the florist's.*

The seated characters – all except HARRIET *(and* CANDIDA*) – are poring over their copies of a dossier, handed out by* HARRIET *as part of a game she has devised. (*HARRIET *is looking pleased with herself. Her game has captured her guests' imaginations.) The audience watch as they digest what they are reading.*

HARRIET   You all look baffled.

PAUL   Give us a chance, Harriet!

JACK   I need to focus.

CANDIDA   Yes, you do.

PAUL   Another drink, Jack?

CANDIDA   Jack's had more than enough.

JACK   Didn't realise I was dating my mother. *(he
               signals to* PAUL *for a refill. The others continue to
               study their dossiers)*

STEPHANIE   *(eventually)* So Lord Manningham's body
               was found in the billiard-room, which
               sits adjacent to the orangery. Bludgeoned
               to death, presumably with the missing
               Chinese vase. How rare was this vase
               anyway, do we know? Those details can be
               important.

HARRIET   There speaks the advocate. Getting to the
               heart of the matter.

STEPHANIE   *(real affection for* HARRIET*)* An advocate on a
               rare night off, thanks entirely to you.

PAUL   But do we *know* the vase is the murder
               weapon? It could have been taken by the
               attacker. If it really is rare, I mean.

Sighs and shrugs – they are stumped. They read on, flipping pages.

CANDIDA   Well, I think it was the gardener.

HARRIET   *(enjoying this)* Why the gardener, Candida?

CANDIDA   I don't know. I just do.

JACK   Having assimilated all the available information without bothering to look at it.

CANDIDA   I've looked.

STEPHANIE   Quick to master her brief.

JACK   You can't just go with a hunch though.

PAUL   Why not? *I* have, now and then.

JACK   And look where that got you…

PAUL looks uncomfortable. Sees HARRIET looking at him and shakes his head at her – there's nothing to be discussed.

STEPHANIE   Maybe the gardener was in cahoots with the poacher. Lord Manningham was on to the poacher – only a matter of time before he rumbled the truth.

CANDIDA   Maybe he was the one stealing from the wine cellar – vintage Bordeaux fetches top dollar.

JACK   It's certainly pricy enough in the restaurants you like me to take you to, my sweet.

CANDIDA   That's the mark-up.

JACK   *(to PAUL)* You were in the wine trade for a bit, Paul, weren't you?

PAUL   I dabbled.

HARRIET   As in most things.

PAUL   *(nettled)* What's that supposed to mean?

STEPHANIE *(before HARRIET can answer)* Would the gardener know how to sell stolen wine though?

PAUL   *(his irritation towards his wife deflected)* What about the vicar? He'd already had a tour of the wine cellar so he knows what's there.

JACK   The clergy are old soaks in my experience – all that blood of Christ.

CANDIDA   When did you ever go to church?

JACK   They come to the casino – in mufti, mind.

STEPHANIE Plus the church roof needs fixing and there isn't the money.

HARRIET   *(picking up the empty cafetière)* I'll leave you to mull it over while I top this up. *(she exits)*

PAUL   And speaking of topping up... *(he gets up and moves around the table, checking who needs their glass replenishing)*

JACK   It's a cigarette I need. And some thinking time.

CANDIDA   They'll kill you, you know.

JACK   Something has to. *(he checks he has his cigarettes and lighter and leaves by the other door, the one leading to the front of the house rather than the kitchen)*

STEPHANIE   Means, motive and opportunity – that's what they say, isn't it, John?

REBUS   They used to in my day.

They turn and acknowledge REBUS's presence for the first time.

CANDIDA   MMO, I like it.

PAUL   What about the brother though? Doesn't he seem a bit too good to be true? And there's been no love lost between him and Lord Manningham since they argued about the witch woman he started dating.

CANDIDA   Madame Violet? Vampire rather than witch.

PAUL	Well, she got her teeth into the poor brother. *(the joke is weak, with a reaction to match)*
STEPHANIE	The two of them together maybe? There's nothing to say we're dealing with a single killer.
PAUL	Hedging your bets? Come on, Stephanie, you're the lawyer. Surely you've worked it out by now.
STEPHANIE	And John's a detective but he's yet to share any startling insights.
REBUS	Maybe I'm holding back. And I'm a *retired* detective, don't forget. Replaced by box-ticking and gender awareness courses.
PAUL	Stephanie's right though, John. This must be meat and drink to you.
REBUS	I've had plenty of both tonight, thanks to you and Harriet.
PAUL	Well, the dinner party was Harriet's idea – and once she gets an idea...
STEPHANIE	I only ever see her at the gym. The number of times I've invited her to lunch or a cocktail...
PAUL	She's not much of a one for gadding about. And the house needs so much looking after.

CANDIDA   *(to PAUL)* So which one of you invited Jack, Paul?

PAUL   Harriet thought it would be nice to meet him in the flesh.

STEPHANIE   And hiring a chef for the night?

PAUL   *(puffed up)* Brendan was all my idea, I'm proud to say.

CANDIDA   Brendan? *That* Brendan? From Jack's casino?

STEPHANIE   *(to PAUL)* You chose well. Everything was just perfect.

CANDIDA   *(looking towards the door to the kitchen)* Is it too late to say hello? Maybe when Harriet comes back.

REBUS   *(steering them back to the game)* Thing is, in my day we didn't find ourselves investigating too many murders in country piles owned by Lord and Lady Whatsit.

CANDIDA   I think you'll find Lady Manningham owns it outright – lived there before she remarried.

PAUL   *(exasperated)* I honestly haven't a clue. Harriet came up with the whole thing. Threw herself into it.

CANDIDA	Impressive. She should be able to monetise that. There's bound to be a market.
PAUL	She reckoned it might be a bit of fun.
STEPHANIE	She's maybe misjudged our sleuthing abilities though.
REBUS	*(at the bookcase)* Not particularly a whodunit fan. I'm seeing Sherlock Holmes and Edgar Allan Poe, and that's about it. Unless you're the reader, Paul?
PAUL	I leave books and art to Harriet.
REBUS	So where do your interests lie?
PAUL	I watch TV, especially sport.
REBUS	*(has been expecting more)* Is that it?
PAUL	I work long hours most days.
REBUS	I bet you do. Investments, you said? Property? Adding more steel and glass to the poor old Edinburgh skyline?
PAUL	Whatever brings in an honest bawbee, John.
REBUS	Looks to me like honesty pays.
PAUL	Mostly, I'm what's called an angel. I invest in start-ups in the hope of a return at some point further down the line.

REBUS   You're a gambler then?

PAUL   *(raw nerve touched)* It's only gambling if you
           don't know what you're doing. *(quoting)*
           'Speculate to accumulate'.

CANDIDA   *(to PAUL)* Isn't that how you and Jack met?
           One night at the casino? Before my time,
           of course.

PAUL   You make me sound ancient.

STEPHANIE Compared to Candida, most of us are.
           (bringing them back to the game again) The
           vicar is a large man, isn't he? From his
           description, I mean. And the footprints
           outside the orangery are a size 10. But
           then the gardener isn't exactly petite.

PAUL   Do the footprints even belong to the killer?
           What sized feet did Lord Manningham
           have?

REBUS   Probably the same in death as in life.

STEPHANIE You need to enter the spirit of the game,
           John.

PAUL   *(raising whisky bottle)* Unless you'd rather opt
           for a different kind of spirit?

STEPHANIE The tiny details can be the most
           important.

REBUS   Though they can make you miss the bigger picture. *(he has turned his attention to the art on the walls)* These are nice.

PAUL   Nice? They're the crème de la crème.

REBUS   Worth a bit then? *(REBUS goes to touch one of the frames)*

PAUL   No touching – most of them have alarms fitted.

STEPHANIE Harriet's very proud of her Scottish Colourists. Am I right in saying it's the finest collection still in private hands, Paul?

PAUL   That's what Harriet always says.

CANDIDA Motive's what we should be looking for, isn't it? Could they have had financial worries? The problem with old money is that there seldom seems to *be* any – it's all tied up in land and the constant repairs of those big draughty houses. My parents were old money, taught me a lesson – give me new money any day of the week.

REBUS   Was that what attracted you to Jack?

CANDIDA *(looking offended)* What makes you think it wasn't love at first sight? *(she sees the look on his face)* Only teasing – Jack's wallet was certainly no deterrent.

STEPHANIE   *(reading her dossier)* You might be on to something, Candida. The bank manager had visited Lord Manningham first thing that morning – meaning it was urgent.

CANDIDA   Jack's the only person I know who still uses a bank – with a proper office, I mean. Face to face meetings over a whisky. He says they're less likely to lie to him when he can stare them in the eye. *(wistful)* I like being around people who have money.

REBUS   *(patting his pockets)* Then maybe I should apologise.

PAUL   Don't tell me you didn't get a decent pension from the police?

REBUS   Depends what you mean by decent.

PAUL   Thirty years' service, you said. Gold watch and all that.

REBUS   And now my time is my own.

CANDIDA   If you'd been a bent cop, you wouldn't have to worry about money.

REBUS   *(slyly)* And what would you know about bent cops, Candida?

CANDIDA   *(realising she may have said the wrong thing; drawing the word out)* Nothing.

REBUS   Jack told you a few things, has he? Or
             maybe he just doesn't realise you're
             listening in on his business while
             apparently busy with your phone?

STEPHANIE   *(stepping into what is becoming an awkward
             conversation)* You do miss the job, John. No
             use denying it. If they wanted you back,
             you'd jump at the chance.

REBUS   Jumping's not really in my repertoire.

CANDIDA   Health is important though – health
             and lifestyle – *(casting an eye over REBUS's
             physique)* especially for men of your age.

REBUS   I grew up in a time before health and
             lifestyle. *(he is next to the bouquet of flowers
             now, fingers playing over the elaborate wrapping)*

CANDIDA   Yes, I can believe that.

*HARRIET enters with the refilled cafetière. Momentarily taken
aback as she sets eyes on REBUS.*

HARRIET   I've been so flustered today I've not had
             the chance to unwrap them.

STEPHANIE   A secret admirer, Harriet?

HARRIET   I just thought they'd add something to the
             room.

PAUL	*(a hint of jealousy)* But then Brendan arrived and your focus was elsewhere. We were discussing motive. I have to say, I'm beginning to question yours. *(he sees she looks anxious)* What's the matter? Is something wrong?
HARRIET	I looked for Brendan in the kitchen but there's no sign of him. He can't have gone, he promised to tidy up.
PAUL	Maybe you frightened him off. You were practically salivating when you described him in his whites. All those little visits to the kitchen during the meal...
HARRIET	*(making an effort to ignore this)* What were you saying about motive?
PAUL	This little game of charades of yours.
CANDIDA	Is that what it is? I've been trying to describe it to my followers. *(she sees REBUS's quizzical look)* On Instagram.
STEPHANIE	Candida did explain it to you, John. She's an Instagram influencer.
CANDIDA	Not just Instagram – all the available media platforms.
REBUS	You mean there's more than one?
STEPHANIE	*(to CANDIDA)* I doubt you'll find any evidence of John on Instagram or Facebook, or anywhere else for that matter.

CANDIDA   Oh my God.

REBUS   Instagram sounds to me like a dealer who
              makes speedy deliveries. We actually had
              a guy back in the day, arrested him half
              a dozen times. Called himself Sellagram
              Tam...

CANDIDA   *(having checked her phone)* No Twitter, no
              Snapchat – you're not anywhere!

REBUS   Except right here, grounded in what I
              like to think of as reality. *(aside to himself)*
              Unlike some...

CANDIDA   I could set you up on YouTube, you'd be a
              genuine curiosity. I'm serious – maybe I'll
              write a blog post. You're like a unicorn.

REBUS   Pretty much how I felt towards the end of
              CID, the last of a very old breed.

PAUL   *(to HARRIET, who is pouring coffee for those who
              want it)* Any chance you can give us a few
              extra clues, darling? Your game has got us
              well and truly stumped.

HARRIET   Maybe later.

REBUS   I never said I was stumped.

STEPHANIE   Yes, you've got that look. I remember it
              well from your days on the force...

The action freezes and lighting changes, maybe a sound
effect to signal what is about to occur. REBUS *walks through*
the room, pausing at each character as he addresses the
audience.

REBUS   'Read the room' – it's a phrase that gets
             bandied about these days. Someone, usually
             a politician, says the wrong thing – strikes
             the wrong chord – and it's because they've
             failed to read the room. The room being the
             court of public opinion. But when you're
             a detective, you DO read the room, quite
             literally. That's what Stephanie meant. The
             living-room, the office, the alleyway. You
             study it and you begin to notice things,
             certain subtle truths, staring you in the
             face. Just look at this place with its art and
             books and fancy flowers. It's telling a story,
             as are its current inhabitants, of course,
             all playing a game of some kind, maybe
             even games plural. Stephanie brought me
             here tonight as part of a game, and I came
             because ... well, I used to think there was
             a spark there. Maybe, old fool that I am,
             I still do. And our hosts, so wealthy that
             their idea of a takeaway is to buy a chef
             and install him in front of an Aga. The air
             crackles between them when they speak ...
             Then there's Candida – just because she
             seems all surface doesn't mean she's not

playing a game of her own. As for Jack
Fleming, well, he's the reason I agreed to
come, and I'm probably the reason why
he'd rather be out on the doorstep, cold as
the night is. Jack's done well for himself
by breaking any number of laws and
trampling those who dare to get in his way.
He's well due a reckoning...

*The action resumes, JACK entering, shaking the chill night
air from him – or making show of doing so.*

JACK   Beautiful sky, crisp and clear. So are the
                charades done and dusted?

HARRIET   You didn't see Brendan, did you?

JACK   Quiet as the grave out there. I've never
                liked that about the New Town – you
                come here at night and it's like everyone's
                hiding. Done a runner, has he? Paid in full
                upfront? *(HARRIET nods)* Mug's game. *(back to
                the game)* So was it the boozy butler?

PAUL   We were wondering if the wine was maybe
                purloined rather than quaffed.

JACK   *(pointedly to PAUL, who is raising a glass to
                his lips)* It's much the same thing to some
                people – people who'd rather others paid
                their tab. *(the meaning is implicit: PAUL has run
                up a sizeable tab at JACK's casino)*

STEPHANIE   *(again, trying to steer the conversation away from conflict)* I have to say, Harriet, the heroine of your story could be based on you.

HARRIET   What makes you say that?

STEPHANIE   Well, she's sporty, plays tennis and hockey. You once told me you played hockey at school. And you're always promising me we'll play tennis one day...

REBUS   But then that would make the victim Paul.

CANDIDA   Well that can't be right. *(she glances at the notes)* Drinking heavily and spending too much time at the village pub, where he's chummy with the rough-edged landlord. *(she breaks off, meaningful look towards JACK)* Oh, I see what you mean.

JACK   What makes you think I'm not the handsome brother who now stands to inherit?

CANDIDA   But then that would make me the vampire woman!

They look towards HARRIET.

HARRIET   *(nervous laugh)* It's just a game.

CANDIDA	M'lady's closest friend is an antique dealer – didn't you say you collect antiques, Stephanie?
REBUS	Does that make me an antique?
CANDIDA	It makes you the detective, John. Except there is no detective.
REBUS	Which makes the scenario slightly less than plausible – apologies, Harriet. But in the real world the professionals immediately take over. Scene of Crime Team, Major Incident Squad, fingerprints and forensics, evidence-gathering and interviews.
CANDIDA	*(still looking at her phone)* So, Mr Expert, help put us out of our misery.
REBUS	The missing vase is the key – I think we can agree on that. But is it a fortuitous murder weapon, or the reason the murder happened in the first place? How valuable was it and was it insured?
STEPHANIE	Attempted insurance fraud? The last recourse of those in dire financial straits...
CANDIDA	*(looking up from her phone)* And strictly speaking, Jack, it's not charades – that's where you mime something and your team has to guess what it is.

JACK	*(nodding)* Used to be on the telly. Una Stubbs and Lionel Blair.
CANDIDA	I loved Una Stubbs. She was in Sherlock.
JACK	She was. And Lionel was Tony Blair's dad. *(CANDIDA narrows her eyes; she knows he is lying/teasing)* Not that you'd know who Blair was either.
CANDIDA	Labour Prime Minister. Fought an illegal war in Iraq. Born here in Edinburgh and schooled at Fettes College.
JACK	How do you know all that? No, don't tell me – you follow him on Instagram?
CANDIDA	John has no presence, can you believe that?
JACK	I can believe most things of people like John. *(to REBUS)* But good on you – if it wasn't for the casino I'd steer clear, too, but it pays to advertise, and I'm the public face so I suppose I'm obliged.
HARRIET	How is your casino doing, Jack? I've given up trying to get Paul to take me.
JACK	*(to PAUL)* You need to stop hiding Harriet away, Paul. We've a nice restaurant you could treat her to, as you well know. Or isn't it refined enough for your good lady? New chef's bedded in, if that's what's

worrying you. Food is back to where it was before Brendan slung his hook. *(to HARRIET)* It's a classy place, Harriet, trust me, as befits an owner at the top of his game. Anyway, you'd be welcome any time. You might even change Paul's luck.

An awkward moment

HARRIET   *(to PAUL; a hint of steel)* I thought you told me you tended to win?

JACK   *(too heartily, after an awkward pause)* He does – that's what I mean! He'll break the house one of these days – if I don't break his fingers first. *(he laughs, PAUL attempting to join in. Slight discomfort in the room at the mention of violence. CANDIDA gives a look that says PAUL's gambling prowess is far from the truth. HARRIET seems to suspect this, too, now)*

PAUL   *(thinking he's off the hook)* Lady Luck, Jack – always put your trust in her.

STEPHANIE The victim liked gambling, too. *(she holds up her dossier)* After-hours card games at the pub, rolling home late. More like you all the time, Paul.

PAUL   *(brushes this off with a fake laugh)* Ready for a malt or maybe a brandy, Jack? How about everyone else? Time for a top-up?

(he checks but the various bottles are mostly empty) Some host I make – back in two ticks. *(he leaves by the door to the kitchen)*

REBUS   So your casino is bucking the trend, Jack?

JACK   What trend?

REBUS   I thought betting was all virtual these days. I sometimes wake up with the TV still on and every advert's for online gambling.

JACK   I make enough to get by. Besides, a physical casino is more of a lifestyle choice.

REBUS   That word again.

JACK   You don't just go there to have a flutter. It's got a bit of razzamatazz, a bit of glamour. It's theatre and music and food and drink.

REBUS   Which is fine until the poor punter goes home and finds himself broke.

JACK   Come and see for yourself some night. Pile of chips on the house.

REBUS   Brown sauce or vinegar?

STEPHANIE   How did you get into gambling, Jack? Casinos, I mean.

JACK   I thought I told you?

STEPHANIE   *(shifting slightly – he is referring to pillow talk,*
             albeit from long back, but something she'd rather
             was kept hidden from the others) Maybe I've
             forgotten.

JACK   I started off with one bookmaker's,
             just one. Ended up making a name for
             myself, expanding. A casino seemed the
             logical next step. Axminster carpets, flock
             wallpaper, proper champagne. Pure class.

REBUS   I always reckon you can't buy class off-the-
             peg.

JACK   Which is why my suits are tailor-made. I
             can give you his name if you like?

STEPHANIE   *(intake of breath; it's all getting a bit tense)* It's
             been a fabulous evening, Harriet. I'm so
             glad you invited me to see how you live.
             And now I'll have to put in a bit more
             effort at the gym to work this off. *(she pats*
             her stomach)

HARRIET   I do love the gym. Paul's always having
             a go at me for spending more time there
             than here. Nonsense of course ...

STEPHANIE   And it's not as if *he* doesn't gallivant.

CANDIDA   I use a TikTok exercise regime. Three
             minutes a day to wellness. *(to REBUS)* It's
             another social platform, very useful for
             influencers.

JACK   Christ, don't get her started on all that
              stuff...

CANDIDA   *(ignoring him)* First you have to lead the
              sort of life your followers don't. Upmarket;
              sophisticated; just about attainable if they
              really really try. You give them lots of little
              glimpses...

JACK   Hence the twenty thousand photos on her
              phone.

CANDIDA   *(ignoring him again, showing her phone screen
              around the table)* For example, here I am
              showing my followers each of tonight's
              courses. See all those little hearts? Seven
              hundred and ten for the scallop starter.
              (she checks the screen again) Twelve...
              fifteen... twenty-five – still climbing.

JACK   Don't ask me how, but she makes decent
              money from it.

CANDIDA   It's not rocket science. Once you're a name,
              companies come to you to help them get
              noticed online. They'll comp you clothes
              and cosmetics, travel and holidays – you
              name it.

REBUS   So basically you're in advertising?

CANDIDA   Influencing, John.

REBUS   It's a different world.

CANDIDA   *(to HARRIET)* Is it OK to mention to my
           followers that you used a chef, or shall I
           say it was all home-cooked?

JACK   *(to CANDIDA)* I told you on the way here,
           a bit of discretion would make a nice
           change.

CANDIDA   I'm not naming names or anything. I've
           not even posted a picture of the house.

JACK   So all those loo breaks during the meal,
           you weren't snapping photos of the
           hallways and staircase?

CANDIDA   Swear to God.

JACK   *(coldly)* Or nipping to the kitchen to catch
           up with Brendan?

CANDIDA   If I'd known he was there I might have.

HARRIET   *(attempting to defuse the situation)* I *can*
           actually cook, I rather enjoy it, but Paul
           argued that it would lead to me spending
           all day in the kitchen, so he suggested
           Brendan. Actually, a free advert might be
           just what Brendan needs. He's not long set
           up on his own, according to Paul.

JACK   I told him he was taking a big risk
           leaving the casino. It was Paul who told
           him cooking for private clients was a
           gold mine. Mind you, I'd probably have

ended up firing him anyway – a record of 'inappropriate conduct'. *(he is staring at* CANDIDA*)*

CANDIDA   *(her dander up)* One drunken snog, Jack. One. And months back at that. Can't a girl enjoy herself?

REBUS   *(enjoying the growing animosity between* CANDIDA *and* JACK*)* This Brendan sounds an interesting character.

HARRIET   Well, he was the perfect gentleman with me. *(to* CANDIDA*)* His company is called Brendan's Fare. F-a-r-e. I'm sure he'd appreciate any help. *(she shares a look with* JACK – *she has taken sides in this 'war', *CANDIDA*'s side to be precise.* CANDIDA *types the name into her phone)*

REBUS   If you're looking for a replacement chef, Jack, I'm at a bit of a loose end. I used to cook once upon a time. Might be why my wife left me – only so many fish fingers a woman can take...

They fall silent, awkward at REBUS*'s glib confession.* PAUL *returns with a couple of bottles and starts replenishing glasses.*

PAUL   Neither hide nor hair of Brendan.

PAUL offers wine to HARRIET. She places a hand over her glass, but he removes it.

PAUL   Let your hair down for once, Har. You might even enjoy it.

STEPHANIE   *(defending her friend)* I think Harriet's enjoying herself fine, Paul.

HARRIET   *(attempting levity)* It's OK, Stephanie. Paul's right, it's not as if I have to drive home after.

PAUL   That's my girl. *(he fills her glass and moves on to CANDIDA)*

JACK   *(to PAUL)* We were just discussing Brendan actually. And how you stole him away from me. *(flustered, PAUL spills a little wine)*

CANDIDA   Clumsy.

JACK   I seem to think you even bankrolled him, Paul. Would that be right? And now here you are rubbing my face in it.

PAUL rubs at the spilt wine with a serviette.

PAUL   He was never going to be happy preparing serving after serving of steak and chips, Jack.

CANDIDA   (taking the bottle from PAUL and pouring for
            herself) Hand/eye coordination, Paul. You
            should take up a sport.

PAUL   I did think of joining a gym, not that long
            back actually.

REBUS   Keeping an eye on Harriet? It seems to be
            the only time she's let out on her own.

STEPHANIE gives REBUS an admonishing look. He is being
as subtle as a doorpost.

PAUL   (awkwardly) Harriet's free to live her own
            life.

STEPHANIE   I'm glad to hear it. The days of chaining us
            to the stove or duster are long gone.

CANDIDA   I can't remember the last time I cooked
            anything.

REBUS   Reckon I could become an influencer with
            my fish fingers, Candida?

CANDIDA   (taking him seriously) On TikTok maybe. If
            you did something amusing with them.

JACK   (surface levity but definitely having a dig at
            REBUS) Maybe get your wife to re-enact
            leaving you while you dish them up. (this
            earns him a dark look from REBUS)

PAUL has moved on to STEPHANIE with the wine.

STEPHANIE   I won't, thanks. *(she has lifted cigarettes from her bag)* Comfort break.

REBUS   I didn't know you still smoke?

STEPHANIE   I'm a woman of mystery.

JACK   Good idea – mind if I join you?

STEPHANIE   I do mind actually. Need to check my messages. *(she holds up her phone)* Privacy required.

JACK   Some juicy trial in the offing? I've not seen any smoke signals.

STEPHANIE   That's good – means the system is still just about functional. *(she exits through the door leading to the front of the house)*

JACK   *(to REBUS)* Know something we don't, John?

REBUS   About what?

JACK   Her latest case.

REBUS   She's a woman of mystery, didn't you hear? – these days at least, eh, Jack?

JACK   *(choosing to ignore the question)* You and her been going out long?

REBUS   We're not going out at all.

JACK But you used to?

REBUS Did we? Not really. Cops and lawyers just get thrown together sometimes, same as lawyers and their clients. Anyway, these days I'm on hand if she needs a plus one. That's all there is to it.

JACK Friends without benefits, eh? *(to HARRIET)* Did you know we'd have a copper in our midst, Harriet? Is that where the after-dinner entertainment comes in?

REBUS Is that what I am?

JACK Don't flatter yourself – I meant the game.

HARRIET I'd no idea John was a detective until he introduced himself – Stephanie didn't divulge who she was bringing. I suppose it has added a certain... dimension. I was going to have us dress up as various characters. Role-playing. But I thought it might be too much like hard work.

JACK I can just see Candida in a little maid's outfit.

CANDIDA Dream on, buster. I'd rather be the widow who stands to inherit.

REBUS Willing to kill for it?

HARRIET That's rather a leading question, Inspector.

CANDIDA   How much are we talking about?

REBUS   *(to HARRIET)* How much are we talking
           about, Harriet?

HARRIET   I hadn't given it any thought. There'd be
           no inheritance tax, so it's not as though
           Lady Manningham would have to sell the
           manor house.

JACK   Happy marriage, was it? I notice they
           don't have kids. You don't either, do you?

HARRIET   *(sharing an awkward look with PAUL)* No, well...

PAUL   Never really saw the point. They grind you
           down, don't they? *(to REBUS, trying to change
           the subject)* You'll have seen a lot of changes,
           John? No more *Dixon of Dock Green* – now
           it's all staring at computer screens.

REBUS   That's true.

PAUL   Cyber crime and online stalking...

REBUS   Yet when it comes down to it, human
           nature hasn't changed. Most crimes still
           boil down to the seven deadly sins. I'm
           sure Harriet's whodunit is no different.

HARRIET   Pride, lust, greed... *(she falters)*

JACK   Sloth?

PAUL   Envy's one, isn't it?

HARRIET	*(watching* PAUL *pop a grape into his mouth)* Gluttony...
CANDIDA	That's five.
REBUS	Six actually.
HARRIET	What are we forgetting? Pride, lust, greed...
REBUS	Wrath. The red mist killers often say descends on them.
CANDIDA	*(suddenly interested)* How many killers have you met?
REBUS	Probably more than I think. Maybe the same goes for you. *(he means* JACK*)* One more thing...
JACK	Yes, Detective Columbo?

Smiles and chuckles around the room; fingers wagged at REBUS *as if to say 'he got you there'.*

REBUS	There are always some who think they'll get away with it. They think they're too smart to ever be caught, or too important to face prosecution even if they are.
HARRIET	But all these new technologies, don't they make it much more difficult to escape justice? Crimes present *and* past?

REBUS   They do, which is why I'm all for them. A
          case might go unsolved for years or even
          decades until something turns up that
          brings everything into focus. *(he is referring
          to JACK, trying to unsettle him)*

PAUL   Can't say I'm too happy about all the
          surveillance these days – your phone and
          computer spying on you…

CANDIDA   It's just a case of tweaking your
          preferences. Never allow 'all cookies'. I
          mean, unless they're the ones *I'm* offering.
          My brand partners are hand-picked. Oh,
          and always cover the camera on your
          computer with a piece of tape – a sticking
          plaster does the job.

REBUS   *(after they've all taken a moment to digest this)*
          All the surveillance in the world can't
          compete with a copper's nose – a copper
          like our friend Columbo. Some of the guys
          I learned from, they could read a criminal
          as if he were a book open at the index. The
          way a suspect acted, their little facial tics
          and tells, the sweat forming on the brow, a
          slight tremor entering the voice. *(he is now
          focussing on JACK, who is exhibiting none of
          these as yet)* I worked with a guy once who
          had the sharpest instincts I ever saw. Bill
          Carter, his name was. If Stephanie were
          here, she'd tell you.

JACK   Why bring up Bill Carter?

REBUS   Why not?

JACK   Because there's a bit of history there, as
              I suspect you know. *(to the room at large)*
              Bill Carter was an utter shite of a human
              being. Got it into his head that he was
              going to put me behind bars, even if he
              had to break every rule in the book.

CANDIDA   *(innocently)* Is this to do with your wife?

JACK   *(angrier)* No, it bloody isn't! *(composing
              himself, mindful of his surroundings)* A man I
              barely knew, a Glasgow man, did a runner
              one day and Carter decided to point
              the finger at me – without a shred of
              evidence.

REBUS   No hard evidence, certainly. But mud does
              have a way of sticking to you, always has
              done.

*An uncomfortable silence. HARRIET stares at PAUL as if
only now realising the sort of man her husband has been
cosying up to.*

JACK   I repeat – no evidence. Then or now.

REBUS   Just a copper's instinct.

HARRIET   *(interested, but also trying to calm things)* But who was this man, Jack? The one who disappeared?

JACK   He was called Ray Collins. Owned a string of gaming arcades on the west coast. Rumour was, he'd run up a mountain of debt and headed for sunnier climes.

REBUS   It's hard to disappear though, isn't it? And not turn up again, I mean. The other rumour current at the time was that he'd been about to make a move into Edinburgh, open his own casino, right here on your patch, Jack – and bigger, classier than the competition.

JACK   Not a grain of truth in it.

REBUS   No truth in the story about those mountains of debt either. Plenty of money left to his estate. *(he turns to CANDIDA)* Why did you bring up Jack's wife?

CANDIDA   Well, she died, didn't she?

JACK   *(still irritated, but also now reflective)* Ten years ago.

HARRIET   Such a tragedy, Jack.

JACK   *(regaining a measure of composure)* I'll never forgive myself.

HARRIET	Just horrible.
PAUL	Devastating.
JACK	Aye, that's the word, Paul – devastating. And it still is, all these years later.

The room goes quiet for a moment, during which STEPHANIE *re-enters.*

STEPHANIE	*(jokingly)* Did somebody die?

JACK flinches, leaps up and leaves the room by the same door.

	What did I say?
CANDIDA	He was just remembering his wife.
STEPHANIE	Oh Christ. *(to JACK, offstage:)* I'm sorry, Jack!
CANDIDA	She drowned, didn't she?
STEPHANIE	Swimming-pool of their villa. Too much booze. Jack wasn't able to save her.
REBUS	I'm sure he found a consoling shoulder. *(he means STEPHANIE, as she well knows)*
CANDIDA	Not mine. I was years away from meeting him.
PAUL	*(to REBUS)* Is all of that true? About that man Collins?

REBUS   You're better asking Stephanie. *(STEPHANIE
                 looks surprised at being mentioned)*

PAUL   *(to STEPHANIE)* Why's that?

STEPHANIE   *(recovering a measure of poise)* I assume we're
                 talking about Ray Collins? *(PAUL and REBUS
                 both nod)* There was a court case. I mean,
                 Mr Collins's family thought he was owed
                 money when he disappeared.

PAUL   Owed by Jack?

STEPHANIE   There was no proof, no paperwork. A
                 gentlemen's agreement, they said.

HARRIET   You seem to know an awful lot about it.

STEPHANIE   I was on the team.

PAUL   The legal team?

HARRIET   No, the curling team – she's a lawyer, Paul!

PAUL   *(to STEPHANIE)* Prosecution or defence?

STEPHANIE   Defence. I was defending Jack.

PAUL   They sued Jack? Ray Collins's family?

STEPHANIE   No, there was nothing like enough
                 evidence to bring a case. I was defending
                 what happened next. An... associate of Mr
                 Collins was sent to Edinburgh – to Jack
                 – with the intention of... applying some
                 pressure.

REBUS	Mad Malky Chisholm.
PAUL	He sounds nice. So where does the courtroom come in?
STEPHANIE	Jack was accused of assaulting Mr Chisholm.
PAUL	Ah.
HARRIET	*(all but clutching her pearls)* And did he? Assault him?
STEPHANIE	*(with an advocate's discretion)* Mr Chisholm was taken to A & E after falling down a flight of stairs.
REBUS	A flight of stairs wearing steel-toed boots.
PAUL	Bloody hell...
STEPHANIE	*(annoyed by REBUS)* I don't remember you being anywhere near that case, John.

REBUS shrugs.

HARRIET	So Jack was charged with the assault?
STEPHANIE	Chisholm wasn't talking and Jack denied any involvement. But a detective called Bill Carter pursued him.
CANDIDA	Bill Carter. *(to REBUS)* That's who Jack and you were talking about.

REBUS nods. STEPHANIE has put the pieces together now.

STEPHANIE   Jack was charged and taken to court – but
              we had an excellent team and the case had
              no merit.

REBUS   Not proven.

STEPHANIE   Bill Carter appeared to be conspiring
              against my client on a number of unproven
              fronts. The judge wasn't happy at having
              his time wasted by a witch-hunt.

HARRIET   *(to PAUL)* Just as well you've not cleaned out
              his casino yet, Paul – doesn't sound the
              sort of man you want to get on the wrong
              side of.

PAUL   *(defensively)* Jack's all right. More than that,
              he's a loyal friend, sticks by you. Anyone
              need a top-up? John, you've been nursing
              that red for a while – fancy changing up a
              gear to a fine malt?

REBUS   Aye, why not.

PAUL   And there's still cheese in the kitchen if
              anyone's hungry.

HARRIET   Plus the grapes, if Paul's not guzzled them
              all. Gluttony is the one sin we seem not to
              frown on these days. *(to STEPHANIE)* While
              you were out, John was telling us the

seven deadly sins are still the main reason people go to the bad.

STEPHANIE Gluttony, envy, sloth ... *(she begins to struggle)*

CANDIDA *(quickfire; eyes still glued to her phone screen)* Pride, lust, greed and wrath. *(the others are surprised by her; she beams a brief smile in their direction – people have underestimated her in the past)*

STEPHANIE So which do you reckon was responsible for Lord Manningham's demise? And is the vase really as crucial to the puzzle as John thinks?

CANDIDA Wouldn't it break? I mean, you hit someone with it hard enough to kill them?

REBUS You'd be surprised how little force a blunt object needs in order to crush someone's skull.

CANDIDA It's always a servant, isn't it? The revenge of the lower orders on their entitled betters. Can't say I blame them. Doesn't do to scrutinise where a lot of inherited wealth comes from. Usually means grinding down more than a few innocent people. Hence all those statues coming under attack and buildings renamed.

She has not looked up from her phone so cannot see the
fresh surprise on the faces of those around her. They are
having their minds changed about her.

HARRIET   Was social influencer your first career
           choice, Candida?

PAUL   Rather than political activist.

CANDIDA   I always wanted to run my own business.
           My parents were keen to help but
           lacked the wherewithal. Besides, I was
           determined to prove myself – sink or swim.
           When I went freelance I formed a limited
           company – decided not to bother going the
           offshore route – the tax savings have to be
           balanced against the amount of attention
           HMRC pays you. I suppose I could have
           stayed Schedule D self-employed but I took
           my accountant's advice. A few more fees to
           pay, being a company, but there are perks,
           too. *(she breaks off and holds up her phone)*
           Salmon main course has seven thousand
           views now. A few thumbs downs from
           vegans though. Doesn't do to get on the
           wrong side of them...

HARRIET   We were talking about cyber-stalking
           earlier. Being so... available... online, do
           you ever have any problems?

CANDIDA   *(blithely)* Dick pics, you mean?

HARRIET   Do I?

CANDIDA   I've had my share. Any woman on the 'net
           is going to get those.

HARRIET   Good heavens.

STEPHANIE It's sadly true, Harriet. Middle-aged
           lawyers are not immune. Mostly they go to
           my office e-mail. If we bother to trace them
           it's usually ex-clients or friends of and a
           warning suffices.

CANDIDA   But then you get upskirters, too.
           Nightclubs are notorious but it can happen
           anywhere – getting out of a taxi, standing
           on an escalator...

*REBUS and PAUL share a look, this is unknown territory to
them.*

HARRIET   It really is another world.

CANDIDA   You need to be careful at that gym you
           and Stephanie go to. Prime location for a
           bit of voyeurism.

HARRIET   I doubt my leotard would find too many
           admirers.

CANDIDA   You'd be surprised. Whenever I post
           a photo in a bikini or sportswear, the
           messages come flooding in, some sicker

than others – and I don't mean sick in a good way.

REBUS Is there ever a good way to be sick?

STEPHANIE Youth speak, John. *(to CANDIDA)* You can report them, you know.

CANDIDA Oh, I do – sometimes. And I block and I block and I block. But they just open a new account, hide behind a fresh avatar, and I'm back to square one.

PAUL What does Jack say about it all?

CANDIDA Used to be, he'd have a meltdown. Want to smash them all in the face. So I stopped telling him – not good for his blood pressure.

HARRIET How did you two meet?

CANDIDA In Venice.

HARRIET How romantic.

CANDIDA He was on business and I was doing a photo shoot.

HARRIET You were a model?

CANDIDA Sweet that you'd think that. But I did work in fashion – executive assistant, that sort of thing. The photo shoot was all very *Death in Venice*.

HARRIET	You know the film?
CANDIDA	Of course – who doesn't?
PAUL	What film? *(he looks to* REBUS, *who just shrugs)*
CANDIDA	Giudecca. Jack was staying at the Cipriani.
HARRIET	*(wistfully)* My first husband took me there on our honeymoon ...
PAUL	*(raising his glass)* Callum, of blessed memory.
HARRIET	I've not been back since.
CANDIDA	The photographer was paying me a bit too much attention. This was as the shoot was finishing. You know what Italian men are like. Jack was at a nearby table and noticed. He marched towards us, holding a wine bottle by the neck. Didn't say anything, didn't need to. The look he gave was enough. *(she breaks off)* Would a wine bottle qualify as a blunt instrument? Maybe one of the ones missing from the cellar? *(she picks up her dossier.* PAUL *and* HARRIET *do the same. As they begin to read, muttering theories to each other,* STEPHANIE *signals for* REBUS *to join her away from the table. They will talk together in a slight undertone)*
STEPHANIE	Is Jack the reason you agreed to come?

REBUS   I seem to remember you wanted me here
               so I could give you my impression of the
               host and hostess.

STEPHANIE   Maybe so, but your eyes lit up when I
               mentioned that Jack would be here, too.

REBUS   Bill Carter went to his grave without
               getting the one result he craved.

STEPHANIE   Jack's wife died in an accident. Malky
               Chisholm was a walking disaster area.
               End of.

REBUS   Maybe.

STEPHANIE   How about Harriet and Paul – or have you
               been too focussed on winding Jack up?

REBUS   I'm on the case, Stephanie, fear not...

PAUL   *(noticing them)* Is this team-work? The forces
               of law and order solving the hideous crime
               behind our backs?

REBUS and STEPHANIE return to the table.

STEPHANIE   We were just wondering what we might
               have missed.

REBUS   Speak for yourself.

PAUL   You think you know the answer, John?

REBUS   Let's wait till Jack comes back. *(he picks
          up a dossier. To HARRIET:)* It's very well done.
          Have you ever been a writer?

HARRIET   Goodness, no.

REBUS   *(gesturing towards the art on the walls)* A
          painter maybe?

PAUL   *(has been standing behind HARRIET; he grasps
          her shoulders, more tightly than she seems
          comfortable with)* My dear darling Harriet
          has never needed a paying job in her life.

HARRIET   *(wriggling free)* The paintings in here are by
          the Famous Three – Corbie, Amberson and
          Drinnan. They were Callum's passion. He'd
          amassed a sizeable collection even before
          we married. This house was his parents' –
          they passed it on to us when they could no
          longer manage the stairs.

PAUL   It all costs an arm and a leg to insure, too.

REBUS   Yes, you mentioned the alarms.

PAUL   Frankly, give me cash over art any day.
          (backtracking, sensing HARRIET's displeasure)
          Not that they're not lovely. Callum had a
          good eye. I mean ... *(gestures towards a beach
          scene)* That one of the south of France.

HARRIET   *(pointedly)* Colonsay actually.

CANDIDA   I get invited to openings sometimes. Video installations; performance art – I like a lot of it.

PAUL   I'm betting Jack doesn't.

CANDIDA   No, he's a philistine, much like you. Not that he's ever on the guest list. I think this is the first time we've ever been invited anywhere as a couple – so thank you, Harriet.

HARRIET   *(a growing warmth between them)* You're very welcome, Candida.

CANDIDA   So what happened to him, your first husband? If you don't mind me asking.

HARRIET   A heart attack.

PAUL   Burned the candle at both ends did Callum.

CANDIDA   *(to PAUL)* You knew him?

PAUL   One of my oldest and dearest friends. I was knocked for six when I heard. Dashed round here to offer Harriet my support and, well, things progressed from there.

STEPHANIE   *(intervening to support HARRIET)* I wish we were doing your game justice, Harriet. You obviously put so much into it. Floorplans and sketches, all the plotting and the character biographies ...

HARRIET   It was actually a lot of fun.

STEPHANIE   The orangery though...

HARRIET   Yes?

STEPHANIE   Well, it leads to the billiard room. Rather than heading outside after the killing, could the culprit have moved further into the house?

CANDIDA   The carpet's described as beige though – and no muddy footprints.

REBUS   *(to* CANDIDA*)* Are you still happy with blunt-force trauma? It's the obvious answer, of course, but *(to* STEPHANIE*)* you've seen the same cases as me, Stephanie – autopsy might tell a different story. Say he'd been poisoned. Poisoned just before, I mean. Whoever bludgeoned him couldn't know that. Their blow knocked him out but it's the poison that killed him.

CANDIDA   And Madame Violet would know all about poisons!

PAUL   So the murder weapon we're looking for might not be the murder weapon?

REBUS   One thing I've learned, take nothing and no one at face value. Healthy scepticism is like an antidote. Having said which, oftentimes the obvious conclusion turns out to be the right one.

STEPHANIE   I get the feeling John is toying with us. It's one of the many traits that make him hard to like.

REBUS   Along with?

STEPHANIE   Smugness for one thing. And holding others to a higher standard than you set yourself.

PAUL   You're being cross-examined, John.

REBUS   And I plead guilty as charged. Tell me, how long was it before you two married?

PAUL   From cross-examination to interrogation!

HARRIET   Six months. A short wooing.

PAUL   *(defensively)* But it's not as if we started as strangers. We knew one another pretty well.

HARRIET   I'm not sure back then I even knew who *I* was, never mind anyone else. *(she looks at PAUL, who stares back. The temperature in the room has dipped. PAUL pours himself another drink)*

PAUL   *(to HARRIET; irritated)* This game of yours hasn't quite worked out, has it? Too tricksy. What you should have had was

something more straightforward – a bit of
music or something.

CANDIDA   Something to dance to! I love being on the
dance floor, as long as it's not with Jack –
the way he moves is embarrassing. I've got
a video. *(she checks that the door is closed;
JACK is not about to come in)* Take a look. *(she
finds the video on her phone; REBUS takes the
phone from her and looks at the screen)*

REBUS   I see what you mean. Is this Jack's
casino?

CANDIDA   A club in Dubai. I got comped for the
whole trip. Probably should have left Jack
at home. As he gets older, the heat gets
harder for him.

REBUS   *(swiping the phone's screen)* Is this the same
trip?

CANDIDA   The hotel was six-star. I mean, beyond five.
Rafts out in the water with sunbeds on
them. Plus iPads so you can order drinks.
The waiters swim out with your order on
an inflatable tray. The water was so blue
and lovely, I couldn't stop posting photos.

*The phone is passed to STEPHANIE, who shares what she
can see with PAUL and HARRIET.*

HARRIET   He really doesn't suit those trunks, does he?

PAUL takes the phone.

PAUL   Budgie-smugglers! I'm surprised he didn't make you delete these. They're not exactly flattering.

CANDIDA   Which is why I'd never put them on social media. I mean, don't get me wrong, Jack looks OK when he's dressed.

PAUL   *(studying one photo in particular)* You do wear a bikini well, Candida, no one could say you didn't.

CANDIDA   Yes, no one ever has.

JACK opens the door and enters tentatively. CANDIDA *snatches her phone back.*

PAUL   We were about to send out a search party... *(JACK downs the nearest drink, rubs the back of his hand across his mouth)* What's wrong? You look like you've seen a ghost.

CANDIDA   *(noticing something is very wrong)* Jack?

JACK   *(after a further moment)* There's a body. Upstairs. Head smashed in... blood... *(he shakes his head, robbed of speech)*

PAUL   What?

CANDIDA   You're kidding.

HARRIET   Don't joke, Jack.

JACK   Do I look like I'm joking?!

REBUS   *(businesslike)* Whereabouts exactly?

JACK   Master bedroom. The en-suite.

HARRIET   Brendan?

REBUS   I need you all to stay here. I'll go see.
            (he pauses at the door. Gives CANDIDA *– and
            her phone – a warning look)* Just don't, OK?
            *(*CANDIDA *nods and* REBUS *exits by door to front
            hall)*

PAUL   This can't be happening.

HARRIET   *(echoing her previous question)* Brendan?

STEPHANIE   *(to* JACK*)* Jack, what the hell?

*JACK shakes his head, refills his glass, sits down heavily
on a chair at the table.* CANDIDA *is unlocking her phone.*
STEPHANIE *reaches a hand out to stop her.*

STEPHANIE   Best listen to John. This is his show now.

*The room goes silent, the actors seemingly in shock as the
lights go down.*

End of Act One

Act Two

Only the briefest of moments has passed since Act One ended. Setting and characters as before. Everyone on stage except REBUS.

HARRIET   *(to JACK)* I don't understand. Are you sure?

JACK   I know a dead body when I see one. *(he breaks off, having said too much)*

PAUL   But who the hell is it?

JACK   I didn't get a close look – face down on the tiles ...

HARRIET   It has to be Brendan.

CANDIDA   Not necessarily. Maybe an intruder. Brendan heard or saw something, confronted them, and fled afterwards.

PAUL   I suppose that's feasible. I mean, there's no other reason for Brendan to be in our en-suite. *(to JACK)* Come to think of it, what were *you* doing there?

JACK   *(with a shrug)* Having a nosy.

CANDIDA   He does it all the time. My underwear drawer's never the way I left it.

STEPHANIE   *(with distaste, to JACK)* Jack!

JACK	*(to CANDIDA)* You'd be advised to keep that gob of yours shut! I knew it was a mistake bringing you.
CANDIDA	So why did you? Why not one of your 'hostesses' from the casino? Micro IQs to match their micro dresses.
JACK	Don't tempt me. *(he pauses, stares at STEPHANIE. His tone softens as he explains)* At first I thought it was just going to be the four of us, nice and cosy. You, me, Paul and Harriet. I was looking forward to that. But then when Paul said you were bringing a date, I knew I had to even things up. *(CANDIDA is looking at STEPHANIE too now, wondering if there's history between JACK and her)*

When CANDIDA starts tapping at her phone, STEPHANIE snatches it away.

STEPHANIE	You heard what John said!
CANDIDA	I wasn't going to tell anyone – not yet. I'm not stupid.
PAUL	When was the last time any of us saw Brendan?
CANDIDA	Mine would be in the casino.
JACK	Same here.

PAUL   You sure about that, Jack? You didn't feel
              the need to confront him, give him a piece
              of your mind? Kitchen's a bit too close to
              here, you might be heard. Upstairs on the
              other hand...

JACK   (prickly) I haven't set eyes on him since he
              left my employ. You on the other hand...

PAUL   I hardly saw him to say two words to. I
              was in the shower when he arrived. He
              was focussed on the food when I got the
              bottles from the fridge.

STEPHANIE   So you did see him?

JACK   Happy with the price you were paying
              him, was he? Didn't maybe try angling for
              more or he'd down tools?

PAUL   Nothing like that.

JACK   Then maybe *you* were the last person to
              see him, Harriet?

HARRIET   Well, maybe... I suppose.

JACK   Stephanie?

STEPHANIE   What?

JACK   Any history with our muscle-bound hunk
              of a dead chef? (STEPHANIE shakes her head)
              For the record, the suspect is shaking her
              head.

CANDIDA   If I'd known he was here, I might have
           said hello.

JACK   Oh, I don't doubt it. And we've only got your
           word for it that you didn't do exactly that
           on one of your supposed trips to the loo.

PAUL   Look, Jack, the only one of us here with
           any reason to wish ill of Brendan is you
           yourself.

JACK   I'm not sure I like your tone, Paul. A
           tone like that might call for a few home
           truths.

   PAUL *is silenced.*

HARRIET   What do you mean, Jack?

JACK   Paul knows. Favours owed et cetera.

CANDIDA   One of Brendan's things in the restaurant
           was, he liked to come out and chat with
           the diners. Did you ask him not to,
           Harriet?

HARRIET   I don't think it came up.

CANDIDA   Maybe he meant to, but then ... *(she
           gestures upwards – Brendan's death got in the
           way, she means)*

HARRIET   You're saying that was maybe why he was
           killed? So he didn't blurt something out at

the table? All three of you knew him. *(she means PAUL, JACK and CANDIDA)*

STEPHANIE   Actually... *(they all look at her)* I've just been thinking about what Candida said. I did get taken to dinner once or twice – to the casino I mean. And the chef did put in an appearance.

CANDIDA   A kiss on the back of the hand?

STEPHANIE   Now you mention it, yes.

CANDIDA   Mmm. *(she is lost in a momentary reverie – Brendan obviously did the same to her)* And there I was thinking I was special.

JACK   *(dismissively)* Anything in a skirt – Brendan was never fussy. *(he sees the looks CANDIDA and STEPHANIE are giving him)* Present company excepted, obviously.

CANDIDA   You, Paul, regularly leaving to fetch more drinks... Harriet, you in and out with the food... Jack and Stephanie and their cigarette breaks... any one of you could have met up with Brendan.

JACK   Don't leave out your good self. As far as we know, you're the only one who let the corpse grope her arse in a pantry.

*CANDIDA stares daggers. The ensuing awkward silence
in the room lasts a good five or ten seconds, everyone
suspecting everyone else. REBUS re-enters by the door to
the kitchen rather than the door he used previously.*

REBUS   Blunt force trauma.

CANDIDA   Just like the game!

REBUS   *(waking his phone)* I took a picture of his
face. As good as I could manage without
moving him too much. *(to HARRIET)* Are you
OK to take a look? *(she nods and he shows it
to her. All eyes are on her and it takes her a few
moments to come to a conclusion)*

HARRIET   *(trying to recover a vestige of composure,
perhaps also slightly relieved)* It's not Brendan.
Thank God.

REBUS   You're sure? *(he shows the screen to PAUL)*

PAUL   *(defensively)* I hardly said more than hello
to him. I was in the shower when the
doorbell rang. Everything was in the swing
by the time I came back down. I got some
drinks from the fridge...

REBUS   *(interrupting)* Alibis aren't what I'm asking
for right now. You knew him. You booked
him for tonight.

PAUL   I just wanted to help him.

REBUS   Prise him away from his previous
         employer, you mean?

PAUL   Anyway, that's not him.

STEPHANIE   So where *is* Brendan?

CANDIDA   *(to REBUS; shrewdly)* You left by one door and
           came back by another.

REBUS   Not much escapes your attention. And why
         did I do that?

CANDIDA   To see if both doors led to the staircase.

REBUS   Bingo. *(he is tapping a number into his phone)*
         Meaning any of us could have gone
         upstairs.

PAUL   What are you doing?

REBUS   This whole house is a crime scene. *(he holds
         the phone to his ear)*

PAUL   Well, I for one am leaving the scene. I need
         a breath of air.

REBUS   *(sternly; professionally)* Nobody leaves this
         room.

PAUL   You can't keep me here – it's my house!

HARRIET   Strictly speaking, Paul, it's *my* house, and
           I think you should do as John says.

CANDIDA   *(to REBUS)* You really think it was one of us?
             Why not Brendan? He's the one who's done
             a runner.

REBUS   He's on my list. *(REBUS's call is answered)* Yes,
             hello. My name is John Rebus. I need to
             report a suspicious death. I've checked for
             a pulse and I can't find one. The address
             is 75 Heriot Row. *(listens)* No, it's not a flat
             – very much a main door property. Scene
             of Crime team and a police doctor needed.
             (listens) No, but I used to be. Quick as you
             can, please. You've got my number if you
             need me. *(listens)* Many thanks. *(he ends the
             call)*

PAUL   How long till they get here?

REBUS   Not long. Depends if it's a busy night.

PAUL   How busy can they be?

STEPHANIE   Not all of Edinburgh is like Heriot Row,
             Paul.

PAUL   So we're stuck here until then?

STEPHANIE   Just as I was about to have a cigarette.

JACK waves his pack at her, offering.

REBUS   No one's going outside – not until the team
             gets here.

HARRIET   But what if we need...?

PAUL   There's a dead body upstairs, Harriet. Surely to Christ you can control your bladder. *(he notices that REBUS is holding something, studying it)* What's that?

REBUS   The deceased's debit card.

STEPHANIE   Was that wise, John? Tampering with the crime scene?

REBUS   Wisdom was seldom mentioned in my annual review. His name's Alan White – mean anything to any of you?

PAUL   Never heard of him.

HARRIET   Me neither.

STEPHANIE   That name rings a vague bell... *(she glances towards JACK)*

CANDIDA   Want me to do a search?

REBUS   Why not? Just make sure that's all you do, eh?

CANDIDA holds her hand out towards STEPHANIE, who, with slight reluctance, hands her phone back to her.

What about you, Jack? Alan White?

JACK   You sound like you might be the one who knows him.

REBUS   *(playing with* JACK) I might have done – not
               known him exactly but heard his name.
               Long time ago... *(he turns his attention to*
               STEPHANIE) Why don't you enlighten us,
               Stephanie?

STEPHANIE   *(after taking a moment to weigh things up)*
               Probably not the same man – too much of
               a coincidence. But there was a detective in
               Glasgow with that name. He was on the
               investigation looking into Ray Collins's
               disappearance. He had dealings with DI
               Carter here in Edinburgh.

REBUS   Is that right?

JACK   You already knew, didn't you?

REBUS   Bill Carter bequeathed me all his case-
               notes when he died. Hundreds of pages of
               neat handwriting and neat theories.

JACK   Meaning supposition and rumour? He
               always saw what he wanted to see.

REBUS   *(brushing this aside)* You might say I've
               retained an interest in the case.

STEPHANIE   The Ray Collins case? Why didn't you tell
               me? *(*REBUS *shrugs)* But you never knew
               Alan White yourself?

REBUS   No, but you did – and so did Jack here.
               Ray Collins's disappearance, then the near-
               fatal beating given to Malky Chisholm...

STEPHANIE   An allegation dismissed by the court.

REBUS   You'd know better than me, Stephanie.
               Alan White stood in the witness box in
               front of you. In front of you, too, Jack.
               Want to take another look at the photo?
               Maybe this time you'll recognise him.

JACK   Ancient history, Rebus. Back when the
               force had more room for bent coppers.
               Besides, you lot always looked the same
               to me – stale and sleekit and pasty-faced.
               (meaningful pause) No offence.

HARRIET   *(to REBUS)* Let me see if I understand. Are
               you saying this detective came to the
               house tonight because of some connection
               to Jack?

REBUS   I'm saying it's a strange sort of
               coincidence. What do you think, Stephanie?

STEPHANIE   I'm not sure what I think.

REBUS   There you are in court, doing your best
               to instil doubt in the jury's minds, using
               all your prodigious debating skills to chip
               away at every witness and each bit of
               testimony, eventually securing the result

you've been paid for – paid terrifically
well, I'm betting. You and your client, long
evenings spent planning your lines of
attack, weary afterwards, easier to check
into a hotel than trudge home...

STEPHANIE *(angered by this)* A fantasy concocted by
your friend Bill Carter. That's what he
left behind for you, John – his febrile
imagination, along with his obsession.

CANDIDA *(reading from her phone)* White's finished
with Police Scotland. I've got a couple of
photos from his retirement do. Looks like
he still lives in Glasgow. Divorced with
a grown-up son. *(pause as she studies her
screen)* Cute-looking. Set himself up as a
private investigator seven years back –
father rather than son, I mean. His contact
details. *(she shows REBUS the screen of her
phone. He allows himself a moment's excitement
– reads from CANDIDA's phone screen. There is a
phone number there for the detective agency. He
taps the number into his own phone)*

STEPHANIE Won't it just go to his mobile upstairs?

CANDIDA It's a landline.

REBUS The type of job where out-of-hours contact
isn't unusual – gives us a reasonable
chance. *(he listens, his face grows less*

animated) Answering machine. *(listens a moment longer)* Hi there. My name is John Rebus. I need to speak to someone urgently about Mr Alan White. My number is *(he gives his mobile phone number)*. I stress again that this is urgent. I'm ex-Police Scotland, the same as Alan, and I'm calling from Edinburgh – a house on Heriot Row. I'm hoping that will mean something to you. Please call me back as soon as you get this message. *(he repeats his phone number and ends the call)*

CANDIDA   *(still reading from her phone screen)* Office off Sauchiehall Street – Glasgow city centre – means he's doing all right for himself. Lives in a flat there, too, by the look of it. Modern penthouse job. Those don't come cheap, even in Glasgow.

REBUS   *(genuine admiration)* Ever thought of coming to work for Police Scotland? We could use a few like you. *Semper vigilo.*

PAUL   What are you on about?

STEPHANIE   The motto of Police Scotland, Paul. It's Latin.

CANDIDA   Always vigilant.

REBUS   Top marks.

HARRIET   *(anxious)* We were all absent, weren't we?
           During the meal, I mean. *(to REBUS)* We
           were discussing it when you were upstairs.
           We thought the victim must be Brendan,
           so we had that wrong, but all the same
           – cigarette breaks and toilet breaks and
           fetching bottles and whatnot. *(to CANDIDA)*
           I have to say it, but you were absent more
           than most.

CANDIDA   No, I wasn't!

JACK   I used to think it was cystitis or something.
           Turns out she just needs regular
           re-preening so she can send another
           pouting snap of herself to her weird fans.

CANDIDA   *(correcting him)* Followers.

HARRIET   *(to JACK)* Then there's you with your
           apparent need for a cigarette every ten
           minutes.

JACK   And each time I went out, I opened the
           front door – I'm sure you all heard me.

HARRIET   So that was your first trip upstairs – the
           one where you conveniently found the
           body?

JACK   Don't start pointing fingers, Harriet. Once
           fingers start pointing, you never know
           where they'll end up.

HARRIET	Yes, you said much the same to Paul. It makes me wonder what's going on between the pair of you.
CANDIDA	Lord Manningham and the local inn-keeper...
PAUL	*(ignoring this tangent)* I doubt he came in by way of the front door anyway – someone would have seen or heard him.
STEPHANIE	Not a window either – all those security precautions you're so proud of, Paul.
CANDIDA	Then he must have come through the kitchen. Brendan would have been in and out carrying stuff, no? Could something have happened to him? How else did this Alan White get past him?

REBUS *thinks for a moment then exits through the door to the kitchen.*

PAUL	Where's he going? *(to REBUS's disappearing figure)* Stay in this room, you said!
CANDIDA	*(to JACK)* Cystitis. God you're such an embarrassment, Jack.
JACK	*(ignoring her; to PAUL)* What the hell have you got me into?
PAUL	This has nothing to do with me!

JACK	Last thing I need is more police attention.
PAUL	Ditto. *(he realises too late what he has said. HARRIET is staring at him)*
HARRIET	*(coldly)* What do you mean, Paul?
PAUL	Nothing, darling.
HARRIET	It doesn't sound like nothing.
JACK	We're just teasing you, Harriet.
HARRIET	Teasing? At a time like this?
JACK	You're quite right – it was in bad taste. My apologies.
CANDIDA	This isn't part of it, Harriet? You and John, concocting this between you? No murder victim upstairs? A pretend phone call to 999? Hang on though… It was you who found the body, Jack. Means you'd have to be in on the prank, and you'd have let something slip. I know you too well.
JACK	Do you now?
CANDIDA	Well, let's just say I know enough.
JACK	And I know about you, too, sweetheart, trust me.

REBUS *enters.*

REBUS   Kitchen's definitely messy. No sign of a struggle though. He either left in a hurry, or ... *(he raises his eyes to the ceiling)*

PAUL   Hidden in one of the rooms upstairs? We should go look.

REBUS   The team will do that. Less we contaminate the house the better. *(pause as they are left to their thoughts)*

CANDIDA   This is more fiendish than your story, Harriet.

REBUS   Well, at least we can clear that up. *(REBUS goes to the bookcase)* Edgar Allan Poe – the one of his I remember best is *The Purloined Letter*, the answer hidden in plain sight, visible to all. *(he walks to the occasional table)* Beautiful flowers – you were too busy to unwrap them, you said, Harriet. But you're a woman to whom details matter. The room was immaculate when we arrived. So there has to be a reason ... *(with a flourish he undoes the wrapping. The flowers are sitting in an ornate Chinese vase)*

CANDIDA   The murder weapon!

REBUS   *(checking the vase)* A smear of blood on the rim ...

HARRIET	Ketchup.
REBUS	*(peers into the vase and removes something)* Looks like the killer dropped a brass button. Maybe torn off in the struggle.
STEPHANIE	Like the ones on the blazer the pub landlord always wears! Why though, Harriet? Why him?
PAUL	Bravo, John.
HARRIET	*(answering STEPHANIE's question)* I'm not sure, to be honest – I just needed it to be SOMEone.
REBUS	But back in the real world – I assume you have a contact number for Brendan, Harriet?
HARRIET	His details are in my phone – but it's charging in the sitting room.
REBUS	Go fetch it then – straight there and back, mind.

HARRIET *exits.*

JACK	No reason for me and Stephanie not to nip out for a smoke then.
REBUS	*(to JACK)* You're staying right here, where I can keep an eye on you.

JACK   You're almost as paranoid as your old pal
              Carter. Bully Boy Bill, they used to call
              him. Not averse to beating a confession out
              of a suspect back in the days when there
              were no cameras. I dare say you did your
              share, too, with Bully Boy as your mentor.
              (he gestures towards STEPHANIE) The reason
              Stephanie tore apart every witness in
              that courtroom is because Carter provided
              her with so much ammo – she ended up
              convincing the jury that it was the cops
              on trial rather than poor humble Jack
              Fleming. Ingrained corruption from the top
              down. *(he blows STEPHANIE a kiss)*

STEPHANIE   *(on the defensive)* I was just doing my job,
              same as I would for any client.

JACK   *(wagging a finger)* You forget, I've seen plenty
              of your colleagues at work over the years –
              you went way beyond, Steph, way beyond.

REBUS   'Way beyond', yes I'm sure. But just
              because she got you off, doesn't mean you
              weren't guilty as charged.

JACK   I'm a simple businessman – ask Paul here.
              I provide dozens of jobs. I work hard. I do
              a hell of a lot more for charity than you
              do.

REBUS   Citizen of the year, eh? Well, let me ask
               you something – how did you get out to
               the raft?

JACK   *(puzzled)* The what?

REBUS   The raft moored off the beach in Dubai
               – waiters swimming out to it with chilled
               drinks – *swimming*, mind.

*JACK glowers at CANDIDA. But this is left hanging as
HARRIET returns. She checks her phone.*

HARRIET   Didn't hear a peep from upstairs. I do hope
               Brendan's safe, wherever he is.

REBUS   If he didn't bump into Jack, he should be.
               (he focuses his attention on JACK) Snooping
               around upstairs. Maybe you came up
               against a face from the past, one you
               couldn't forget because he'd tried so
               hard to pin a murder on you, then gave
               evidence in the GBH case. A copper who
               knew there's no smoke without fire.

JACK   Blah blah blah.

REBUS   *(to the room at large)* It's all in Bill Carter's
               files. All of it. *(he shares a look with STEPHANIE.
               She folds her arms and looks stern – she has
               been used – he's only here because of those
               files)*

STEPHANIE   *(to REBUS)* Some date you are.

JACK   *(to REBUS)* Did you know he'd be here
tonight? Our dead private eye? Maybe
you're the one who let him in.

REBUS   To what purpose? See, that's what we need
to know – why was he upstairs in the first
place? Why here, why tonight?

PAUL   *(remembering the chat from earlier)* Means,
motive and opportunity.

CANDIDA   MMO.

JACK   *(to REBUS)* You knew I'd be here – did you
tell him? *(he watches REBUS shake his head.
Turns to CANDIDA)* Maybe you blabbed then?
Put something on the internet that he saw.
(she shakes her head. JACK turns to STEPHANIE)
You knew him back in the day, didn't you?
And you left the room a few times...

STEPHANIE   I've not set eyes on him since the trial.

HARRIET   *(to REBUS)* Brendan's number. *(HARRIET shows
REBUS Brendan's details on her phone. He taps a
number into his own handset)*

CANDIDA   Shouldn't they be here by now? If this is
all real, I mean?

STEPHANIE   As John says, maybe it's a busy night.

During the following, REBUS *will move towards the door and make his exit while on the phone.*

REBUS Is that Brendan? Brendan, hello – it's good to hear your voice. I'm calling from Harriet and Paul Godwin's. *(the other cast members share looks – relief that Brendan is alive and one mystery is about to be solved)* No, no, no, the meal was fine, no problems on that score. You've left the kitchen in a bit of a state though. I need to ask you about that – and one or two other things...

The door closes behind him. PAUL *rushes over and presses his ear to the door.*

HARRIET Paul!

PAUL *(fiercely)* Shut the hell up, woman!

Sharp intakes of breath from the women – HARRIET'S *sharpest of all.* PAUL, *realising.*

 I mean, it's our house, isn't it – we have a right.

STEPHANIE *(correcting him)* Harriet's house, Paul.

PAUL We're husband and wife, Stephanie – half and half – I'd have thought a lawyer would know that.

CANDIDA   What is he saying? *(she means REBUS)*

PAUL   It'd be easier to hear with a bit of hush.

The room goes silent. CANDIDA and HARRIET join him at the door, listening. JACK and STEPHANIE have come together at the opposite end of the room. They speak in an undertone.

JACK   He knows about us, doesn't he? I mean, obviously he does.

STEPHANIE   He didn't hear it from me.

JACK   It'll have been in those bloody case notes. Hotel security guards are notorious. Half of them are ex-cops and they'd sell their granny's passport for a bottle of Famous Grouse. Why the hell did you bring him along tonight?

STEPHANIE   *(a meaningful look towards the trio at the door)* I needed those sharp instincts of his. But as it turns out, John had an ulterior motive.

JACK   That motive being me.

STEPHANIE   So it would seem.

JACK   *(softening a little)* Look, about what happened ... back then, I mean.

STEPHANIE   I'm a big girl, Jack. You got what you wanted.

JACK	It would never have worked, Steph. Between us, I mean. You must have known that. It's not like I was the first...
STEPHANIE	What do you mean?
JACK	Well, word gets around...
STEPHANIE	How dare you!
CANDIDA	*(noticing them)* What are you two muttering about?
STEPHANIE	*(regaining her composure for the 'public gallery')* The body upstairs – what else? *(she and JACK return to the table, albeit awkwardly. HARRIET and CANDIDA do the same, though PAUL stays at the door, ear pressed to it)*
HARRIET	It really couldn't have been any of us, could it? We're nice people... mostly.
STEPHANIE	As John often says, everyone's fine ninety-five per cent of the time, even psychopaths. On the surface, I mean.
HARRIET	Jekyll and Hyde?
STEPHANIE	Like the killer in your game.
CANDIDA	*(looking at JACK)* The pub landlord.
STEPHANIE	Having felt the need to dispatch Lord Manningham doesn't mean they're likely to kill anyone else. They've dealt with the

one problem that was messing with their equilibrium.

CANDIDA   A friendship soured? Maybe a loan that wasn't being repaid?

STEPHANIE   Whatever the reason, afterwards the killer goes back to being a model citizen, and those around them know no different.

CANDIDA   A model citizen like Jack here, giving so generously to charity.

PAUL   *(joining the others at the table)* He's either gone outside or upstairs. Can't hear a thing. *(to HARRIET)* Sorry about earlier, old girl. Nerves have gone to pot tonight.

HARRIET   Nobody's managed to explain why that man was in our en-suite.

STEPHANIE   Just because he ended up in the bathroom doesn't mean he was attacked there.

CANDIDA   Killed elsewhere on the premises and dragged somewhere more private?

JACK   *(enthused by this idea)* By a killer who needed to keep the body hidden until everyone had gone home. *(his eyes dart between PAUL and HARRIET)* A killer or killers who didn't think anyone visiting would have need to be in that bedroom, that bathroom.

HARRIET   What's that supposed to mean?

PAUL   Don't be absurd!

JACK   Is that what I am, Paul?

CANDIDA   There'd be smears of blood, wouldn't there?
               Across the floor, I mean. From wherever he
               was attacked to where he was found.

JACK   I didn't see any. Just a bit in the bathroom.

PAUL   Why in the world would a private detective
               be skulking around our house in the first
               place? You're the only connection, Jack.

STEPHANIE   Was it the first floor he was interested
               in? The bedroom suggests he was looking
               for valuables. Then there are your upper
               floors...

HARRIET   The whole house is far too large for us.
               But downsizing would mean selling most
               of Callum's collection – and I could never
               do that.

   JACK and PAUL share a look.

CANDIDA   You should sub-divide. This part of town,
               you'd make a killing – pardon my French.

HARRIET   Do you know who constructed this place?
               Its first owners, I mean? They were called
               Lord and Lady Manningham.

CANDIDA   Ha!

HARRIET   I don't know a great deal about them but
            they also had a country pile in Perthshire.
            No doubt they made their money from
            slavery or something equally unsavoury.
            They passed this house on to their son,
            who hosted parties for a spiritualist known
            as Madame Violet. Her adherents were
            known as 'the Hive' and used to drink
            blood.

CANDIDA   She's real? I need to look that up.

JACK snatches her phone away.

JACK   You and your bloody contraption! How the
            hell does the battery never die? *(he tosses it
            on to the sofa;* CANDIDA *goes to retrieve it)*

PAUL   *(eyes on the door)* What's keeping him? *(he
            goes to the door, presses his ear to it again)*

*STEPHANIE approaches HARRIET, places a hand on her
shoulder.*

STEPHANIE   Are you all right?

HARRIET   *(wistfully)* It was meant to be a pleasant
            diversion, that's all. I wanted you to meet
            Paul.

STEPHANIE *(meaningfully, with a look in* PAUL*'s direction)*
And after everything I'd gleaned from
you, I was keen to meet him, too. *(turning
her attention back to* HARRIET*)* I'm a lawyer,
Harriet, as well as a friend. I was
concerned for you.

HARRIET Concerned?

STEPHANIE Sometimes the most important things are
the ones people don't quite summon up the
courage to say out loud.

Before HARRIET *can respond to this, the door opens and*
REBUS *re-enters. He notes that* PAUL *has been standing by
the door.*

REBUS Well, he was ready to deny it until I told
him a man was dead.

PAUL Deny what?

A tense pause prior to the revelation.

REBUS Alan White paid off your chef.

HARRIET Paid Brendan?

REBUS White would pretend to be helping in the
kitchen. That was his cover so he could
recce the house. He then told Brendan he
could knock off early, White would clear

everything up. Brendan was at the end of a long shift, so he agreed. White had given him quite a lot of money.

HARRIET   But I didn't see anyone in the kitchen apart from Brendan – you believe his story?

REBUS   I've no reason not to. He stayed out of the way until Brendan left. After that, he probably headed straight upstairs, bypassing the dining-room. *(pause. A revelation is coming)* White told Brendan he was a private detective, hired by a spouse to find evidence of infidelity.

PAUL   *(aghast)* What?

REBUS   *(to HARRIET)* Hired by you, Harriet.

PAUL   *(to his wife; scandalised)* Harriet!

REBUS   Brendan thought the story plausible. He'd always found you a bit shifty, Paul – sorry I can't sugar-coat the pill. The way you used to hang around the casino, eyeing up the hostesses when you weren't bending Jack's ear...

JACK   *(with a chuckle)* He had the measure of you all right, Paul. *(he shakes his head slowly)* Cheating on Harriet though – that's beyond the pale.

PAUL   Keep out of this, Jack!

JACK   Or what? *(squaring up to PAUL)* Fancy your chances, do you? Well, here I am – I'll even let you have the first punch, how's that? You'll be in hospital before you can throw a second.

PAUL   *(not about to accept that challenge; turning to HARRIET)* I swear to God, Harriet, I'm not like that. I've never… *(disbelieving)* And you paid for a private detective? Paid him to snoop on me in our house? For Christ's sake!

HARRIET   But I didn't! It's not true! Yes, there are times I've thought… *(she breaks off before saying too much)* I mean, I've wondered if you're keeping something from me. And those moments when you lose your temper and nearly… *(turning to REBUS)* But I wouldn't know the first thing about going to a private detective.

REBUS   *(after a moment's consideration)* I'm inclined to believe you.

HARRIET   What?

REBUS   I believe you.

The others take this in.

CANDIDA   So why would he lie to Brendan?

REBUS   Maybe to conceal the real reason for
               wanting to be here.

STEPHANIE   The real reason being?

REBUS   I'm working on that. Candida, can you
               get busy, see if you can dig up any of Alan
               White's recent cases?

REBUS's phone pings a message. He checks the screen.

               Scene of Crime team are here. I'll let them
               in and point the way. All of you, stay here.

He exits.

JACK   *(angrily, to* CANDIDA*)* You enjoying yourself?

CANDIDA   *(ignoring his tone)* Most excitement I've had
               in ages.

JACK   If I'd known this is what turns you on, I'd
               have arranged for a murder sooner. *(he
               picks up one of the dossiers)* Didn't really
               need any of this, did you, Harriet?

PAUL is standing in front of the seated HARRIET.

PAUL   The missing vase as murder weapon – a
               bad husband, drinking the cellar dry
               and spending his nights elsewhere –
               your revenge, Harriet? On me? The

goody-two-shoes brother – is that Callum
by any chance? We were like brothers,
me and him. You didn't know Rebus was
coming, but you'd invited your lawyer
friend. Trying to tell her between the lines,
her or maybe me, hoping I'd change my
ways and bend to your will?

HARRIET   Bend *you* to *my* will? *(she snorts; home truths
coming out. She has grown steely)* I only really
kept you around in the early days to stop
the wolves from circling. *(to CANDIDA)* As
you found in Venice, Candida.

CANDIDA   Wolves aren't so bad sometimes – better
than the alternative, I mean.

PAUL   *(simmering anger)* Well thank you, my dear
wife, thank you very bloody much! To
think I put you on a pedestal!

HARRIET   Is that what you did? Then why does it
feel more like a cage?

PAUL *has no answer to this. He sits down heavily, pours a
fresh drink, a large one.*

CANDIDA   How long do you think we'll be stuck here?

JACK   I told the casino I'd look in on my way
home.

CANDIDA   Most likely meaning you won't *come* home.

JACK   Well, it's not like there's much waiting for me there, eh? Not for a long time.

STEPHANIE   *(answering* CANDIDA'S *question)* They'll probably just take brief statements tonight. Here or at the station. Formal interviews tomorrow. Hair samples and mouth swabs for the DNA. Fingerprints, all of that. For purposes of elimination. *(she pauses)* If you didn't hire him, Harriet, who did? Any enemies or dark secrets? When it's a murder inquiry, you don't want to hold anything back that might come to light later.

PAUL   We're not the type to have secrets. *(to* HARRIET*)* Are we? I mean, not the kind Stephanie means. *Dark* secrets.

STEPHANIE   That would make you unique in my experience.

PAUL   *(almost at the end of his tether)* Well, your experience is the criminal classes – not the New Town; not the likes of us.

HARRIET   Police cars... in THIS street. We'll be pariahs. A retired judge lives next door...

CANDIDA   You'll be the absolute opposite of pariahs, Harriet, trust me. This isn't the 1950s. My bet is, you'll be invited to every dinner party in the city and beyond. You're about to become celebrities. Isn't that the most amazing luck? And it goes for the rest of us, too. *(to HARRIET)* Your first step should be to get an agent.

PAUL   Rather than a lawyer?

CANDIDA   You'll need one of those for the contracts, obviously. But the agent will secure the best price for your story – you won't be hot for long, no one ever is. The agent will whisk you on to the right chat shows, negotiate your fee for any appearances on TV or in the glossies. I know a couple of names I'd probably trust to handle you – I mean, they're sharks obviously, but it won't be you they bite.

JACK   So who are you selling your story to, Candida?

CANDIDA   Right now I'm a bit busy doing as I was told.

JACK   Doing as you're told? First time for everything.

STEPHANIE   You need to start looking like you're cooperating, Jack. No holding back.

JACK   *(sneering)* Is that a friend talking or a lawyer? I've got nothing to hide.

STEPHANIE   I refer you to my earlier answer. *(JACK looks bemused, so she elucidates)* Everybody has secrets.

JACK   Even you, Stephanie. Just remember that.

CANDIDA   People always tell me I'm an open book. The more they think that, the better for me.

REBUS re-enters.

PAUL   Well?

REBUS   SIO will come and talk to us in a bit. Police doctor's up there with the Scene of Crime crew. They'll start photographing and collecting evidence. *(to CANDIDA)* Any joy?

CANDIDA   Joy is a relative concept. Give me two more minutes.

REBUS seats himself on the sofa. STEPHANIE joins him. Their conversation will be semi-private.

STEPHANIE   Are you OK?

REBUS   I'm fine. Just a bit rusty.

STEPHANIE   Doesn't look that way to me. *(she tries to squeeze his hand but he pulls away)* You know, don't you?

REBUS   *(with a look towards JACK)* It was in Bill
             Carter's notes.

STEPHANIE   He had eyes and ears at the hotel? *(she
             reflects on this while REBUS nods)* You know
             what trials are like, John – pressure
             cooker meets trench warfare. Strange
             alliances can form for the duration.

REBUS   You crossed a line though, Stephanie.
             Lawyer copping off with client.

STEPHANIE   Smart young woman meets edgy older
             man.

REBUS   Back then, I thought 'edgy older man' was
             going to be my role.

STEPHANIE   Thing is though, you were never quite my
             type.

REBUS   Not enough gangster chic? *(he is trying to
             make a joke of it, but her words have cut him)*
             Aye, looking back I can see that. You were
             always at your best defending bad boys.
             They put a spring in your step, and now I
             know why.

STEPHANIE   *(giving him a hard look)* Only ever that one
             time, John. What the hell do you take me
             for?

REBUS   Doesn't really matter, does it?

Having cut her just as she cut him, he crosses to the table, joins the others. STEPHANIE follows, albeit slowly, almost reluctantly, his words having done their job.

JACK   I've been thinking – what about Brendan? He takes a bung from the private eye but then changes his mind. Goes in search of him, intent on handing the money back and making him leave. There's an argument, it gets out of hand.

REBUS   And they do this in whispers? Arguments usually involve a bit of volume.

JACK   Solid floors and walls, sturdy doors.

PAUL   Was the door open or closed when you found him, Jack?

JACK   *(thinking)* Bedroom door was slightly ajar – I might not have gone in otherwise. Bathroom door was mostly open.

PAUL   Not much attempt at concealment then?

JACK   Getting your story ready, Paul? Good man. I'd do the same in your shoes.

STEPHANIE   No sign of a weapon, Jack?

JACK shrugs. She turns to REBUS, who shakes his head – no weapon.

HARRIET   I remember a film where a leg of lamb was the murder weapon. Everyone ate it, meaning no evidence.

JACK   How about a Chinese vase? We only have your word for it that you used ketchup. Maybe you should check again, John – evidence lying in plain view, just like you said.

PAUL   You're not really helping, Jack.

JACK   Give me one reason why I should.

CANDIDA   *(eyes on her phone screen)* This is interesting. One of White's cases, he worked with a museum in Glasgow, helped them retrieve a painting that had been stolen in broad daylight.

REBUS *reads from her screen.*

After that, a couple more museums took him on. One in Paris, one in London. He didn't get anywhere those times though.

STEPHANIE   Any purloined artworks hidden under your bed, Harriet?

HARRIET   I think the cleaners would have noticed.

JACK   You do have that big painting above the bed though.

HARRIET	Callum's favourite Amberson. Definitely not stolen from any gallery.

REBUS has been circling the room, the pieces falling into place for him. PAUL may be sharing growingly nervous glances with JACK, JACK's face a sternly composed mask in reply. REBUS's phone buzzes and he answers the call.

REBUS	Hello? *(listens)* Oh yes, yes, thank you for getting back to me – I appreciate it's late. Do you mind giving me your name? *(he takes a pen from the table so he can write on one of the dossiers)* Jane Turnbull. And you work for Alan White, Ms Turnbull? *(listens)* Well, I'm sorry, but I need to share some dreadful news with you. There's been an unexplained death and we have reason to believe that the deceased is Mr White. *(listens for a slightly longer time)* I really am terribly sorry. Is there someone you can call, a friend who could come and be with you? Are you in Glasgow? *(listens)* No, I'm in Edinburgh, at the house on Heriot Row. *(listens)* That's right. Yes, that's the number. Do you happen to know why Mr White came here tonight? *(listens – everyone hanging on his every word and facial gesture)* Hmmm. And the client's name? *(listens)* I appreciate that, but this is a police inquiry and we'd like to get to the bottom

of it – I'm sure Alan would have wanted that, too. *(listens, and writes a name on the dossier)* And would you have a way of contacting this individual, a phone number say? *(listens)* It would be hugely useful, yes. Uh-huh. *(listens – everyone in the room on tenterhooks)* Yes, very relevant, I'm sure. And when did this client start to have doubts? *(listens)* Thank you. That's helpful. You'll be contacted by one of my colleagues to take a proper statement, and if you need me at any time you have my number. I'm sorry again for your loss. Thank you. *(he ends the call)*

STEPHANIE   'Colleagues'?

REBUS   Old habits die hard. *(he shows CANDIDA the name on the dossier)* Think you can work your magic?

PAUL   So what did she say?

JACK   Don't keep us bloody guessing, man!

REBUS   Small tremor in your voice there, Jack? Maybe I should take you up on your offer of a casino visit – game of poker between the two of us. *(to the room)* White came here tonight to do a first recce. My feeling is, when he saw Brendan he realised what was happening and decided he might be

able to get inside the house. He collared
Brendan outside and made the offer. *(he
sees that* CANDIDA *is waving her phone in his
direction. He checks her screen, takes the phone
from her and holds it out towards* HARRIET*)* Do
you know him at all?

HARRIET   *(studying the screen)* Should I?

REBUS   Probably not. *(reading from the phone)* His
name is Elliot Freeman. *(he gauges reaction
around the room. There are shrugs, blank looks)*
No one? Elliot Freeman? *(reads some more)*
Based in London, independently wealthy. A
patron of the arts. In fact, he's a collector
– *(meaningfully)* has a special fondness
for Scottish paintings of the pre-war
period. Names like Corbie and Drinnan
and Amberson. *(he has walked across to the
paintings, studying them as he passes)* Earlier
this year he bought a few pieces privately
– meaning not at auction. According to
White's assistant, Freeman was beginning
to have doubts about their provenance.

STEPHANIE   Doubts? You mean he thought they were
stolen?

REBUS   Actually, at first he wondered if maybe
they were forgeries, albeit very good
forgeries. But he had them checked and
they were the real McCoy, which was odd

because he thought he had a pretty good idea who they'd belonged to. *(he is facing* *HARRIET)*

HARRIET   Me?

REBUS   Not unknown for a seller to want to remain discreet, meaning anonymous. But he'd read in an interview about Callum's collection and how much it meant to you personally. He was mystified, so he decided to dig a little deeper. *(he is studying one of* *the paintings very closely)* He engaged the services of Alan White, an investigator with a reputation in the art world.

HARRIET   I'm still not sure I... What are you suggesting, John? That I'm in league with this Freeman character?

REBUS   *(to PAUL)* Don't get too close, you said, Paul. Alarms, et cetera. Not the only reason not to get too close though, eh?

HARRIET   Leave Paul out of this – those paintings have nothing to do with him. They belonged to Callum – they're all I have left of him!

PAUL   *(has been building up to this, rises to his feet* *in an explosion)* Bloody Callum! Always bloody Callum! They're fakes, woman! These ones. The ones lining your own bloody walls. *(he lifts one painting down from the wall and approaches* HARRIET *with it)* Don't get too close, yes, or you might actually SEE something for a change – if you could ever be bothered to look past your narrow bloody privilege! Do you even see ME any more, or am I just like everything else in this house? A faint echo of Callum, the only man you could ever allow yourself to love? *(he looks at the painting, studies it – then punches a hole through it. Gasps from the onlookers)* Fake. All of them. I knew damned well you wouldn't notice. You'll never know the thrill I got from switching them. It was like I was freeing myself from you and Callum and everything else. And it was so easy to do once I'd—

JACK   *(interrupting, urgent)* Shut the hell up, Paul!

REBUS   Ah yes, of course you know.

PAUL   Know? He's the one who put me in touch with the forger!

JACK   Shut your bloody trap before I—

REBUS   *(to* JACK*)* You won't be doing anything, not with a posse of Edinburgh's finest one floor above us.

JACK   *(to PAUL)* If you hadn't kept racking up
        such huge bloody losses you wouldn't have
        needed the money!

HARRIET *(has been aghast and still is; she takes the ruined
        painting from PAUL, as tenderly as though it
        still holds real value for her)* Forgeries? All of
        them? *(her eyes bore into PAUL's)* There are
        more vampires around us than we might
        think. I always knew you were among
        their number, the way you came fluttering
        along, with Callum still warm in his coffin.
        Always hovering. Accidental meetings that
        were anything but. At any other time, you
        wouldn't have stood a chance. You think
        I'm two-dimensional? Maybe so, but at
        least I'm real. What I'm looking at now
        has always been fake. Slapdash at that, no
        finesse – strictly amateur hour.

PAUL   *(suddenly drained)* I cared about you, or tried
        to. I really did. But I could never measure
        up to Callum, not the way you'd re-cast
        him after death, far from the reality of
        the man I knew, the man he never showed
        you.

Momentary silence. The cast are in shock, mostly.

JACK   Right, to hell with it, I'm out of here.
        Murder Squad know where to find me.

REBUS	I don't think so.
JACK	*(all menace)* Try stopping me. *(he makes for the door but stops when REBUS speaks)*
REBUS	Candida, show me that photo again, will you? The one from Dubai. *(there is a staring contest between JACK and REBUS while she finds it. REBUS speaks to JACK)* She showed it to us when you were out of the room. Lovely picture of you, Jack, nice and relaxed, beetroot-coloured gut hanging over your ridiculous trunks.
PAUL	*(with a measure of venom; any friendship between him and JACK now history)* Budgie-smugglers!

CANDIDA *hands* REBUS *her phone.* REBUS *holds it out for* JACK *to see.*

JACK	So?
REBUS	So when did you learn to swim, Jack? You said at the time you couldn't save your wife because you were scared to death of water. You looked around for a hook or something so you could drag her to the side of the pool, but by then it was too late. Yet here you are, out of your depth on a raft so you can be served chilled drinks on your holiday by waiters who have to swim to you.

CANDIDA   *(disbelieving)* Scared of water? You were in
           your school swimming team, Jack. You
           showed me your medals.

JACK   Shut it.

CANDIDA   You never did exhibit much remorse, said
           the marriage wouldn't have lasted...
           Though you were happy enough with the
           life insurance. Yes, you were very happy
           about that...

JACK   Who the hell wants to listen to you? Know
           what you're good for? Showing your arse
           around the gaming tables, keeping the
           punters well-oiled. Only half a step away
           from the escort you used to be.

CANDIDA   Escort? Only in your grubby little mind. I
           was a PA and bloody good at it, while you,
           mon cher, are good for one thing and one
           thing only. *(she waves her phone at him)* Your
           extensive list of contacts – the legit punters
           from the casino, not your criminal pals –
           all of which are tucked away in here now,
           meaning I can finally kiss you goodbye.

JACK   *(growling)* I can destroy you.

CANDIDA   Not if I destroy you first. Some of the video
           and audio I've got... *(she waves the phone
           again)* Well, let's just say you're lucky John
           here is *ex*-CID.

REBUS   The SIO upstairs isn't though. I'm sure
          they'd be interested in anything you want
          to share.

JACK looks at the faces around him, feeling betrayed. He
grabs CANDIDA's phone and throws it to the floor, stomping
on it for good measure. He stops when he notices
CANDIDA's amusement.

CANDIDA   All safely stored on The Cloud, Jack. Well
          out of your reach.

Silence in the room. HARRIET has walked to the wall and
is staring at one of the remaining paintings, her fingers
brushing its surface. REBUS approaches her.

REBUS   Stephanie brought me here tonight
          because she was worried about you.

HARRIET   *(distantly)* Worried?

STEPHANIE *(in confirmation and consolingly, to HARRIET)*
          Everything you didn't quite say at the
          gym... you painted a picture of a man who
          was overly controlling.

PAUL   I never laid a hand on her!

STEPHANIE Abuse doesn't have to be physical. You
          never liked the thought of Harriet leading
          her own life. You wanted her here,
          swaddled. Your little nest egg.

REBUS   *(to PAUL)* Stephanie is good at reading people – lawyers usually are.

STEPHANIE   But a detective like John sees the big picture.

HARRIET   *(understanding)* And instead of abused and abuser, you find Paul to be little more than a common criminal.

PAUL   *(pleading)* Harriet, please, for pity's sake.

CANDIDA   *(referencing the deadly sins, to PAUL specifically)* Jealousy and greed.

REBUS   *(to STEPHANIE, referring to JACK)* He could swim.

STEPHANIE   *(nodding)* New evidence. Case needs to be reopened.

REBUS   And then there's his role in the forgery. Forgery *and* theft...

JACK   *(at breaking point)* Stuff the lot of you. *(he pours himself a large whisky)* You think you're smart, Rebus, but you're strictly second division.

REBUS   You mean I'm no Bill Carter? I suppose that's true – but I get the job done, no corners needing to be cut.

HARRIET   *(still with questions needing answers)* The detective upstairs – Alan White. Which one of us killed him? Had he worked out about the forgeries? In which case ... *(she points towards* PAUL *and* JACK*)* Or was it to do with the man who disappeared? *(her finger stays pointed at* JACK*)*

JACK   You're not having me for that!

PAUL   Well, I know it wasn't me. Stephanie, you knew him, too, didn't you?

CANDIDA No obvious motive though. Harriet's right about that. *(she joins* HARRIET *in pointing a finger at* PAUL *and* JACK*)*

REBUS   *(enjoying himself)* Just one more thing. *(he smiles; a conscious echo of the Columbo line from earlier in the play)* Sorry, couldn't help myself.

STEPHANIE What is it, John?

REBUS   What if I told you nobody in this room killed Alan White?

HARRIET Then we're back to Brendan again. But you spoke to him on the phone, you seemed convinced of his innocence?

REBUS   Not Brendan either. *(he waits to see if the truth will dawn on any of them.* STEPHANIE *gets there first)*

STEPHANIE *(hesitantly)* Accidental death?

REBUS	*(in confirmation)* Accidental death. He's having a good look around and suddenly he's caught short – you see it a lot with housebreakers. The nerves get to them. He can't risk the downstairs bathroom – steady stream of visitors, plus it's within sight of the front door and therefore anyone stepping outside for a smoke might spot him. But what's this in front of him? A handy en-suite. Marble floor though, still wet from the shower Paul took. White's trainers have flat soles, they make less noise that way. But on a slippery floor... He loses his footing, tips backwards, cracks his head against the corner of the sink. There's a little smear of blood there, just where you'd expect it.
HARRIET	An accident? And you knew all along?
REBUS	A copper's instinct.
HARRIET	But you made us think...
REBUS	You could liken it to shaking the tree, seeing what fruits might fall.
CANDIDA	So none of us is the killer? *(a glance towards JACK)* Not tonight anyway.
STEPHANIE	Just people with secrets, some darker than others.

JACK   *(to PAUL)* You set this in motion, Paul. I
         blame you for this whole mess. Don't think
         I'll forget.

PAUL   I wish I'd never met you. *(he turns towards*
         HARRIET) We were all right, weren't we,
         Harriet? For a time anyway?

HARRIET turns her face away from him, saying nothing.

STEPHANIE Enjoyed yourself this evening, John? *(he*
           offers a modest shrug)

CANDIDA   It'd make one hell of a podcast. *(to REBUS)*
          Promise me you'll think about it.

REBUS's phone has pinged a text, which he is reading.

REBUS   It's from the SIO. Transport's waiting
         to take us to Leith Police Station. A few
         questions to answer. About the deceased,
         and forged paintings, and a suspicious
         drowning. *(to PAUL and JACK)* Casino might
         not be seeing either of you for quite
         some time. *(he opens the door to the front*
         of the house) Don't keep them waiting.
         (the cast begin to gather up their few bits and
         bobs – phones, maybe jackets, spectacles, bags,
         cigarettes. JACK takes a final slug of whisky,
         exhaling loudly. PAUL offers HARRIET his help, but
         she ignores him. Chance here for last looks filled

with meaning – HARRIET and PAUL; CANDIDA and JACK. HARRIET leaves first, followed by JACK and PAUL. CANDIDA pauses on the threshold, turns her head back towards REBUS)

CANDIDA   Call me, John. Call me anytime. *(she exits. Now only REBUS and STEPHANIE are left)*

STEPHANIE   Will you? Call her, I mean?

REBUS   You've got to be kidding.

STEPHANIE   I'm sorry for what I said earlier. About not... *(she breaks off as he waves away her apology)* You've still got it, John. I doubt you'll ever lose it. You should feel proud. *(she exits with a backward glance at him, leaving the door open. REBUS closes it. He is alone on stage now. He takes a moment to compose himself, enjoying the sudden quiet in the room. He pours a whisky and savours its aroma, studies the ruined painting. But before he can drink, he addresses the auditorium)*

REBUS   Between you and me, I'd pretty much finished reading the room by the time the starter was being cleared away. Paul and Jack – I could see something between them, some hold Jack had over Paul that had tempted Paul to cross a line. But I could see, too, that he'd enjoyed crossing that line. No regrets. And Candida? She

was sharp, too sharp for Jack, so why
was she with him? Not for his tough-guy
image, that didn't seem to impress her
at all. But he had friends in high places
as well as low, people who could be
very useful to her as she climbed the
social ladder. Harriet and Paul – well,
theirs wasn't much of a marriage at all,
Stephanie was right about that. Maybe
the fact that Paul is the controlling type
and has a good conceit of himself had been
attractive to Harriet in the early days, but
those days were long, long gone. She was
tired of that life and tired of him. Plus
she knew he was hiding things, lying to
her, covering things up. Probably explains
the dinner invitation – she wanted to see
Paul and Jack in a room together. Would
something slip? Would the truth emerge?
*(he pauses; takes a sip of whisky, rolls it around
his mouth)* Then there's Stephanie. Dear
sweet Stephanie. Still attracted to Jack,
God help her. Not as savvy as Candida
in that regard. Blinkered and beguiled.
(he sighs) Well, John, win some, lose some.
You lost Stephanie a long time back. But
her instincts were correct. Harriet was
unhappy and Paul was the root cause.
And now she's free of him, if that's what
she wants. *(he studies his surroundings)*

Edinburgh at its most gilded and dangerous, a city where vampires dwell. A city full of malice. Yes, malice – that's what Harriet's game was. Her way of telling her story, hoping others would see it for what it was. A game called malice. *(he raises his glass in a toast, drinks again and exhales)* And then there's me, John Rebus. But I'm not a game to be played. *(he gestures towards the bookcase)* Maybe I'm more like a book, a book that's best left closed. I read the room. The room doesn't read me . . .

REBUS *puts down his glass slowly, takes a last look around, maybe lingering on the smashed painting and the others still on the walls. Then he opens the door, exits, closing the door after him with slow deliberation.*

CURTAIN

THE END

An Afterword

A *Game Called Malice* started life during the long days of Covid lockdown. I don't think that's a coincidence. People were confined to their living-quarters for increasing (and increasingly claustrophobic) stretches of time. Some relationships were prone to fray. The world outside began to have less and less meaning. In a quest for social interaction, people planned and hosted Zoom dinner parties and the like. Some of us turned to games and puzzles (mainly jigsaws and cryptic crosswords in my case). I began to muse on the idea of writing something about a small group of people in a confined space, their layers of personality peeling the longer they stayed put.

Back in my student days, one of the few dramas on our literature course was *Who's Afraid of Virginia Woolf?* by Edward Albee. It was an incredible and indelible dissection of one marriage in particular and relationships in general. The threads that bind a couple or a group of friends or a family can be thin indeed, and it doesn't take much to cause them to snap. The film that was eventually made of the play, featuring Elizabeth Taylor and Richard

Burton, benefited from the fact the audience knew that the actors were surviving the stormiest of relationships in the real world. Mostly it played out in one room, over one night, with only four actors.

Then one day during lockdown the film version of another famous play appeared on TV – *An Inspector Calls*, starring the wonderful Edinburgh-born performer Alastair Sim. You probably know the play – it remains a set text in many schools and is a perennial bestseller – but to be honest it had passed me by. This was my first viewing and it astonished me. I began to wonder: what if the family in J. B. Priestley's play lived in a wealthy enclave of Edinburgh? And what if the titular Inspector happened to be called John Rebus? By his very presence, would we begin to witness cracks in the veneer of an apparently happy marriage?

Since I was spending a portion of lockdown life completing puzzles, I decided that there would be a puzzle being played within my play. Years ago I wrote a short story where Rebus is invited to a role-playing murder mystery where participants dress up as various figures in the story and have to work out which one of them is the killer. Whenever I've taken part in these evenings myself, I've proved to be woefully inept in the detecting department. The town of Cromarty hosts a crime fiction festival each year and the local Am Dram Society has been known to put on just such an event. On the occasions I've been present, I have failed to unmask the murderer. Often times I guess too soon – as used to be the case when I played Cluedo. The game in my play – a game called

Malice – would borrow from Cluedo and from the traditional English whodunit. The victim would be a titled gentleman, murdered in his country pile, with a cast of suspects including a clergyman, a gamekeeper, and, yes, even the butler. The play's first act would introduce us to the guests at a refined Edinburgh dinner party and we would watch them try to unlock the secrets of the game while giving away secrets of their own, revealing aspects of their true (and less refined) nature.

I decided on a cast of six for two reasons. One, it seemed a manageable number; and two, to echo the title of Luigi Pirandello's iconoclastic stage play *Six Characters in Search of an Author*. As well as the married hosts of the party, I already had John Rebus, and I knew he would find himself well out of his comfort zone. It made sense that he would not himself have been invited (the hosts being above his pay grade, as it were) but would be someone's 'plus one', that person being a senior lawyer, Stephanie Jeffries. She has invited Rebus for a specific reason, but he has his own agenda which she will only discover as the action of the play progresses.

The two final guests comprise a mismatched couple – rough diamond Jack Fleming and glamorous Candida Jones (the archetypal older man/younger woman scenario). But again, as the evening wears on, we see that games are being played within their relationship and the power may not lie where we would expect it. Six characters, all harbouring secrets, all with histories (sometimes shared) needing to be explored or exorcised. Trapped within a single unchanging set (a townhouse drawing room), all I had to do was increase the heat beneath this pressure-cooker, and as I've found in the past, Rebus is very good at bringing people and events to the boil.

I was not doing all of this alone, however. Thanks to the wonders of the internet and Zoom technology, my co-writer Simon Reade and I thrashed out plot points, rejigged the set and dialogue, and basically brainstormed on a regular basis – without ever meeting in the flesh. Such was life during lockdown. Simon, being a proper playwright, sees problems and potential issues that I don't and the drama benefited from his wisdom.

A Game Called Malice had its world premiere at the Queen's Theatre in Hornchurch in February 2023, the cast being led by the wonderful John Michie as Rebus. That version, however, is not quite the one you have in front of you. The prospect of publication – and future touring for the play – has given Simon and me the chance to revise the original script, adding depth to the characterisation, moving a few more pieces around, and inking in a further red herring or three. There may even be more jokes – there's certainly more tension.

This is my third full-length stage play and the second to feature John Rebus. The fun for me in putting a whodunit on the stage is that the audience gets to play detective in real time. We all become Rebus, sniffing out clues and trying to decide which characters are lying to us and why. When I watched the play in Hornchurch, I got an incredible buzz as the audience responded with gasps and occasional laughter (thankfully only in the right places), and I then enjoyed eavesdropping during the interval as theories and suspects were discussed and mooted over G and Ts and glasses of wine – in a delicious echo of the play's very own first act. I don't remember anyone getting the right answer.

Did you?

Ian Rankin

Production Photography
From The World Premiere
A Game Called Malice
All photos © Mark Sepple

Cast List from the World Premiere
First performed at Queen's Theatre Hornchurch, February 2023

John Michie as John Rebus
Rebecca Charles as Harriet Godwin
Billy Hartman as Jack Fleming
Emily Joyce as Stephanie Jeffries
Forbes Masson as Paul Godwin
Emma Noakes as Candida Jones

John Michie as John Rebus

Billy Hartman as Jack Fleming

John Michie as John Rebus and Emily Joyce as Stephanie Jeffries

Left to Right: Emily Joyce as Stephanie Jeffries, Emma Noakes as Candida Jones and Rebecca Charles as Harriet Godwin

Left to Right: Emily Joyce as Stephanie Jeffries, John Michie as John Rebus, Forbes Masson as Paul Godwin and Emma Noakes as Candida Jones

Forbes Masson as Paul Godwin and Emma Noakes as Candida Jones

Left to Right: Rebecca Charles as Harriet Godwin, Billy Hartman as Jack Fleming and John Michie as John Rebus

Full cast and set